Candids
Snap Shots of the Real Lives of Fictional People

Christine Noble

Lydia;
I hope you see a little
of your story in these.
— Christine N.

1

© Christine Noble, 2014

This book and the individual works within may not be reproduced, in print or electronic form, without the expressed written permission of the author.

Acknowledgements

There are so many people that this book could not have happened without that I do not know where to begin.

I suppose first and foremost I owe a thank you to everyone who has ever encouraged me in my artistic endeavors. I have spent the better part of my life being a coward when it comes to pursuing my dreams, and you have not given up on me.

In particular I want to thank my siblings, Ben and Liz, as much for putting up with my crazy as for their being two of my biggest cheer leaders. There are now long time friends like Chris Manos, and Ben Hale (as well as others) and newer friends like Christine Green and Leala Farnsworth. All people who have believed in me and encouraged me to do the same.

I cannot forget, of course, my sister by another mister, Rachel Doll, or her wonderful husband Aaron, who have been a rock for me for some time now.

One last thank-you, and keeping in mind that I could fill an entire book with those I am missing. This book would have stalled out and taken a good while longer to create if it was not for my most excellent land lady and friend: Lyn Ramsay. When my computer, War Machine, petered out, she let me use hers to keep on blogging and to finish this collection. Candids is not a thing without her, or any of the rest of you, and for that, you all have my undying gratitude (including those of you not mentioned by name.)

For my "little" brother: Benjamin. I think he understands more than most that we are all of us stories.

Foreword

I spent the better part of my creative life thinking I had to create some grand, sweeping story of mythic proportions. I started out, very young, hoping to be the next Tolkien, or at least the next Brooks. To me, for too long, the only stories worth creating were fantasies full of peerless heroes overcoming impossible odds.

A funny thing happened on the way to that destination, one I have not entirely given up. A few years ago, on my blog Hand of Ananke, I started to post flash fiction. It started out as a simple writing exercise; a means to hone my skills. If I could write an even somewhat compelling story in four hundred to five hundred words, imagine what I could do with fifty thousand.

Before long this activity took on a life of its own and I realized something, a fact that should have occurred to me long before, but had not: all stories are interesting.

Everyday people struggle and hope. The challenges of their lives can be monumental, or they can be mundane, but they are there just the same. There are as many stories as there are people in the world, and probably a great deal more than that. Inspiration need not come from the search for a lost magical talisman, though that is sometimes fun, but from the ring of a coffee stain on a table cloth.

I understand many writers have reached that conclusion long before I did, but I was happy to find it just the same. Suddenly what had been a daily chore to keep my skills from atrophying had become a daily delight. I was able to put my mind in the head and heart of another in ways I had not before. These tales were more than an exercise in writing, they were an exercise, I hope, in empathy.

So now I give you a collection of those stories. I present most of the flash fiction, almost all of it under four hundred words, and none of it more than five hundred, posted on HoA over the past three years. Some of the stories involve events of great magnitude for their subjects. Others are simple reflections on daily routines. There are characters who will inspire love, pity, rage, and worry. Depending on your story, they may inspire something different for you. Regardless of what they inspire, I hope you get the chance to think about your tales, the daily, seemingly inconsequential events in your life, and the lives of others, that we so often miss.

Thank you, and enjoy.

Christine Noble; writing from a snowy Brockport, NY.

PIN

The rain patters lightly on the black surface outside, creating a gentle, white noise that makes fighting off sleep harder for Kyle than he would like. He sits behind the cash register in the Kwik-Stop gas station, waiting for the obviously drunken business man to make his selections from the cooler. Staggering to the counter with his blue jacket slightly off his left shoulder the man hands the skinny gas station attendant his purchase, a bottle of sports drink, and his debit card.

He does not mean to pay attention, but Kyle cannot help notice the PIN the man enters. The customer stumbles out the door and into his Mercedes and it is not until the car has disappeared into the night that the card on the counter is noticed. Kyle takes it into his fingers delicately, as if attempting to hold a poisoned needle. The numbers sit at the front of his brain.

Looking across the store, all bathed in fluorescents, he ponders the ATM in the far corner. He thinks about how much he wants a new smart phone, about a better apartment, and he thinks about asking Darlene to the movies. He thinks about his crappy little job, with its crappy little pay, and how he can make it easier for just a little bit.

He is not stupid. He would never use the ATM here in the store. He could take the

bus across town in the morning, take out
what he can, and toss the card into the canal.
No one would ever know. He would never
get caught.

Kyle can imagine the advice Steve would
give him. Steve the ex-convict. Big, burly
Steve with the tattoos, who Kyle tries hard
to convince himself that he does not admire.
He would say the suit had it coming, that
you have to take what you can, and then
Kyle would chuckle nervously and tell him
he is right. He would say Steve is right
because Kyle has always played by the rules
and that has landed him right here, in the
Kwik-Stop, with no hope and less pride.

He grips the little, silver card in his fist for a
moment and with more effort than he would
have imagined pushes it into his front pocket.
Kyle will get a little for himself. He will ask
Darlene to the movies. He convinces himself
he will not feel bad about this, that it will all
work out. He may even believe it.

*

Another First Day

She leans against the tiled wall, watching the
students pass by. In her full length, brown,
corduroy skirt, white blouse and boots she
feels ridiculously overdressed compared to
the young people all around her. Pretending

everything is perfectly fine she takes a deep breath, as if trying to keep her heart from leaping right from her mouth. She closes her eyes for a moment to take another deep breath before clutching her books to her chest and walking into the class room."Excuse me, professor" a tall, tanned, muscular young man in a sleeveless, gray shirt and shorts walks up to her "do we need the Friedman book right away?"

"I… I'm not the professor," she answers softly, trying not to seem too embarrassed, "I'm a student."

"Oh, um, cool." He shrugs his shoulders and returns to his seat.

In her mind's eye they are all staring at her, the old lady in the room. Forty two and only just returning to school after fifteen years away, what must they think of her? She avoids looking at them, and instead concentrates on organizing her notebook, books and other course materials. This wastes only ninety seconds of time, and there are still nine minutes before class begins. All around her the young people chatter, and again the self-conscious, self-absorbed part of her tells her it is about her, though really, she knows that is not the case. This is her reward. This is what she needs after giving up her dreams twice: once to marry her husband and see him through law school, the second time to have their children. Now that their youngest is in middle school, and he can work from home, it is her turn to go after what she wants. She does not feel guilty. She makes herself not feel guilty. She is an excellent wife and mother, but she can be other things besides if she chooses.

The professor comes in and she is certain he is younger than her. The young man walks up to him and they exchange words quickly. It is obvious from the dejected look in his eyes as he goes to sit down that, yes, they will need the Friedman book right away. She takes it from the bottom of the pile and the instructor looks over at her and smiles. All the instincts she has learned as a woman over the years do not like that smile and she brushes her hair out of her eyes, making sure to do so with her left hand to show off her wedding band. His smile fades a bit and he looks out over the class.

"OK, kiddies," he claps his hands, "I am Dr. Weilland…" he goes on about the syllabus and her nerves settle. She can do this. She will excel in her studies, she will not feel old, and she will not feel   guilty.

*

Seven More Days

It has been a long week and Liam is well
past the point of not wanting to deal with it
anymore, but the universe does not work
like that and he knows it. Seven days of well
wishers and sympathizers. Seven days of
well-meaning family politicizing Craig's
condition. "Just imagine if this happened
two years ago," they tell him to show their
support, as if that will bring his husband out
of his coma.

He knows he should not be angry. The small
army of people bringing food, giving him
rides to the hospital, and just being there so
he doesn't have to sit in that gigantic house
all alone are a blessing and he knows it. Still
the mid-morning sun floods Craig's hospital
room and his sister's family hover about
smiling their awkward smiles he wishes they
would just go away. He just wants to hold
his love's hand in peace and have what little
private time they can in between the rush of
nurses, orderlies, and physician's assistants.
The day drags and he nods as a doctor
comes in to explain what they already know,
which is to say, they do not know anything.

No one knows why Craig suddenly passed out at work. Blood work, CT scans, and an endless list of other tests and all they know is he is not waking up. His sister writes all this down and for a moment Liam feels guilty for resenting her presence.

Tara and Teresa, his beautiful nieces, sit on his lap. Tara strokes his cheek, smiling up and him, and promises that Uncle Craig will be alright. He wants to believe so much. He tells her he does and just wanting to makes it happen just a little. The girls' love is reciprocated and rewarded with a big hug before he sets them on the floor. It is almost time to go, so Liam stands up to kiss Craig's forehead.

It has been a long week, and Liam knows next week will be longer still, but he knows, deep down, that they can cope. He knows Craig would carry this burden for him, so he must do the same. After all, they promised each other, their families, and their God that they would.

*

Into The Sunset

They are just five friends: young people
enjoying their last day of their last summer
together. Each young man has known the
others since grade school and now they are
less than twenty-four hours from beginning
their last year of college. New friends have
come along, and while their love remains,
they each accept, to varying degrees, that
they are drifting apart. Things change
whether we want them to or not.

They gather at the county park near Simon's
home on the lake, just sitting in Kyle's truck.
The sun is setting and Simon packs his
favorite, purple, glass pipe before taking a
long hit. He passes it to Mark who passes it
Lonnie. No one offers it to Kyle, that's not
how he rolls and the other four have never
bugged him about it, and he's never judged
them. Simon sets his seat back a couple of
notches and just watches the twilight over
the water. His consciousness fades into a
pleasant fuzziness and he cannot help but
grin a child's innocent grin at the wonder of
it all.

Just an hour or two: this last little piece of
lost time together. They talk about nothing
in particular. No one addresses how it will

be almost a whole year before they see each other again, if at all. All of them are going on to grad school except Mark, who is guaranteed a job in his dad's agency if he finishes school next spring. They will all be too busy this year and beyond to keep touch. Right now, though, none of that matters. The sun is just a sliver on the lake now. However much they avoid speaking about it the reality of their circumstances creeps into each of their minds. Volumes are left unspoken in the pauses between vacuous conversations: an epic poem fifteen years in the writing of mundane stanzas and sometimes broken verse. A decade and a half of first dates, pranks, trophies, fights and reconciliations and it all should seem so pointless on this, the cusp of their first adventure without each other, but they hold on to it for as long as they can. As their buzz fades and the first stars appear, they realize the sun has set.

*

Ticking Away Unheard

He can't get his hair quite right as he fusses in the hallway mirror. It is Nick's first date in over twenty years. In the living room the twins, back from college for the holiday, side eye him. They both think it is too soon. The ink is not even dry on the divorce and here he is going out on a date with some young woman he met at a conference. It is like they have forgotten that it was their mother who cheated on him, apparently for half their marriage.

They don't appreciate him, he knows that. Carol never did. For years, when the twins were toddlers, she complained that he was never home. He should have noticed, he realizes now, when she stopped complaining, but there were contracts to write, clients to please, and ladders to be climbed if he was going to pay for this house and all the comforts they enjoy. His father did the same and he loved him for it. His father appreciated it all, because dad knew the difference.

Growing up in a third story walk up during and after the war, dad would have to endure his father never being there and not having anything to show for it. Opa was a bartender, and apparently everyone loved him. Heck Nick still loves him but he was such an irresponsible goof. He overspent at Christmas, Halloween and Easter. He was great fun, but he and Oma never got out of that walk up. Dad was different.

Dad drove Nick hard to succeed just like he did. He got out of that old building and into the burbs. He loaned Nick the money for college and gave him the drive he needed. That's why he loves his old man so much, even if they never talk, even though he always forgot his birthday. He gave Nick the best gift he could, and now Nick can afford to send his kids to school, even if they waste it on philosophy and dance. Now he can afford to put his dad in the best assisted living community, even if he never visits him there.

He refuses to feel guilty as the twins roll their eyes and he walks out the door. He made his choices and Carol made hers. Nick has worked hard for it all, and might finally let himself enjoy it.

*

Grease Trap

Eight to ten hours a day. That is every Tuesday through Saturday for Jack. That has been every Tuesday through Saturday for him for thirty years. Give or take. Thirty years of blistering heat and cramped spaces. Thirty years of coming home to his wife and kids smelling like a grease-trap. Three decades of wear and tear on a body that complains every time he takes off his shoes now.

He dices tomatoes for omelets without even thinking about it. It's just one of the dozens of tasks that needs to be done between the breakfast and lunch rush. He took five minutes for a cigarette break but that is all he is going to get between now and when the dinner crew comes in. His large gut squeezed between cutting boards on the grill and coolers he grunts as he moves from one prep job to the next. He scrubs his kitchen clean, just as the first five tables or so amble in.

He grimaces and grumbles as servers vent their frustration on him, because of course, yelling at him will make a chicken breast cook faster. He vents back at them and later, if he's not too exhausted and frustrated, he'll feel a little bad about it. After all, they're the ones that have to deal with impatient guests on a schedule. He never got that. If you don't have the time to wait for a proper meal, why not just drive to a fast food joint? Then again, he wouldn't have a job with out these, silly impatient people who get an entire hour off for lunch (and how nice that must be!) Just fifteen more years he tells himself as the headache waxes and wanes at the end of lunch. Just that little bit longer until he can retire, so to speak, and he and Becca can enjoy their "Golden Years." He'll still have to work part-time because there was no way at the wages they have made to really put away. Not if they wanted to send their kids to school. He made darn sure they wouldn't end up like him.

He changes out of his kitchen uniform and shuffles out the door. One more day in the trap, one more day of dull frustration, and he's closer than ever to his reward.

*

Prepackaged

Margaret sits cross-legged on Kenny's bedroom floor, surrounded by clear, plastic totes. The bed is taken apart and stacked in the corner, most of his dresser has been packed away, and a stack of color samples sits in the built-in bookshelf in the opposite corner. She thumbs through one of the totes full of comic books. Ridiculous, really, how much money her little boy spent on all these things. She tries to hold back the tears as memories of his running up the stairs, plastic bag in hand, to jumping on his bed and reading overcome her.

No one ever tells you it is going to be like this. He is not gone, she tells herself, just in Switzerland on his honeymoon before moving into his and his new wife's home across town. Nothing really is changing. He had not lived at home for three years, keeping this room only for visits. Still, it will not be his room anymore. This is the whole point of being a parent, is it not, this moment when you let them go to roam the world on their own? Why, then, does she feel this profound sense of loss?

Sighing as she packs his clothes away she cannot push back the memories of this time or that when she told him to throw this shirt or that away. He kept them, despite fading to the point of being unrecognizable. She resists the urge to put those shirts in the totes that will remain in this house. He will want them for when his gaming buddies come over. They are Taylor's problem now.

This will be the guest room, a place for a revolving door of friends and family to use. Kenny will not need it anymore. He is not

coming home from college. When he visits
it will be for the day, for an hour, for a few
minutes, from just across town, where she
will rarely see him during his busy weeks.
Ken Sr. has plans for this room. He pretends
to not be affected, but Margaret knows
better. Finishing up she puts the comics in
the "for here" stack. Kenny wants his little
cousins to enjoy them when they visit. She
thinks about this, she thinks about
adolescent feet charging up the stairs, and
smiles.

*

Stepping Up

Sweat beads on Peter's forehead, running
down his cheek and dropping of his chin. He
is on his ninth mile now in the summer heat.
His lungs burn just a little, he has been
pushing too hard, and his shins are starting
to shout at him. Just three more miles and he
is done for today. He does not think about
finishing, the shower after, or getting on
with his chores.
In this moment he is in the "zone." Just
aware enough of his surroundings to not get
hit by a car or trip into a drainage ditch.

Nothing else matters, just pounding the pavement: one mile, then a second, then a third, until he has spent his morning exploring the villages and towns around his without looking. The canal trail is the best, where he can just lose himself in the distance.

Every day is like this: training for hours. He came so close last year, just missing the cut to go to states. He wants it, more than anything he has ever wanted. His dad told him he needed to get a job if he wanted a car, so Peter decided he would just walk everywhere, and ride the bus to school. A few odd jobs give him spending money, no time for more than that when there is only time to train.

Deep into his groove now, he is not even thinking about winning now. No, the only thing now is the mountain of time. Time he has to eat up and whittle down. There is too much time and he needs to make it smaller. He needs to improve, just like coach said. "Do a little better each time. That is all I ask." So Peter does. One day at a time, one mile at a time, one hill at a time, and one interval at a time. Each exercise and each meal is chosen to make himself better.

He does not know what winning the state

title will get him. Cross country runners are not the most popular athletes in school. He just wants it, to show himself he can, and maybe see his name in print. Maybe one of the few schools that offer scholarships for distance runners will notice. Maybe he will just keep running. Maybe nothing else matters.

*

Wallpaper Girl

Everyone gathers around the dining room table stretching across the large room with its three extra leafs. At one end is the birthday girl, all smiles as mom and dad set the cake in front of her. Three candles flicker over white icing and around the table, aunts, uncles, cousins, and grandparents cheer, laugh, take pictures and just celebrate the little one's special day. Behind Grandpa Dave, Aunt Katie stands back a few paces, smiling quietly.

Aunt Katie, the one who brings the most gifts, piling them high. Aunt Katie: who always comes alone, no uncle or cousins in tow. She never married. It is not that she did not want to. Yes, Katie is a "career woman", though that label is less shocking than it was when she was little. Still, she had the time, but never seemed to take it. Frightened of rejection, terrified of attention, and worried that she would screw it all up, she never put any effort into finding someone to share her life with, even though it is something she has always wanted.

Her sisters-in-law have stopped trying to hook her up with their cousins and college friends. Katie is happier alone, at least that is what they believe. She does not need anyone else to define her, and in some small way that is true. Contentment has crept into her life. So is now happy, more or less, with living vicariously through her brothers and their families.

It is not so bad. It is fun most of the time. She gets to spoil her nieces and nephews rotten. When an old roommate needs time away from their busy family life she is the first one they call: Katie the free-spirited, Katie the eternally unattached. Still, sometimes that loneliness sneaks up on her, and she finds herself wanting to cry at the most inappropriate moments. Always in control, she never lets it show, shoving it down where it does not ruin someone's wedding, graduation party or baby shower.

Today is different though. It is one of those good days. Happy that little Brianna is turning three she just sits back and enjoys the ride. Today she gets to be fun Aunt Katie, and that, for now, is enough.

*

Acrophobia

Fluorescents fill the tiny office with oppressively bright light and Alan rubs his eyes before tapping away again at the keyboard. Reports to file, spread sheets to proof, and requests to approve or deny (ok, usually it is deny) his life has eased into a dull groove of sameness. Nothing exciting ever happens to him, though truth be told he would have no idea what to do if it did. This is not where he imagined himself, fifteen years ago when he left home for the first time to attend university. He saw ladders to climb, board rooms to wow with his brilliance, and worlds to conquer. He was president of his high school's Future Business Leaders of America, a giant in his tiny domain. How different college turned out to be.
Everyone was brilliant there and by the end

of his first semester, giant Alan was suddenly a gnome. Lost in a swarm of swifter, smarter, busier bees his work was adequate but nothing more. He could not match their energy, and worse, the more he thought about it, the more he did not want to anymore. Attempts to shine ended in embarrassment, so he got by, got along and barely graduated.

A job fair his senior year landed him a job with his current employers. It was low demand, low pay work, but it was a job. Just smart enough, not too ambitious, eager to please, and, most important, afraid to make waves, Alan is his supervisors' dream. A few cursory advancements landed him this office, where he never gets into trouble, where he avoids conflict, and he avoids that now oh-so-frightening ladder.

Not very often he wonders if he could have done something different. He wishes he was not so afraid of this big world he was so hell-bent on diving into when he was younger. Maybe he can still make his mark, but that means standing up, being noticed, and putting your head in the cross-hairs. He is not sure he has the strength; in fact he is certain he does not.

So he ignores it, this aching shame. He hides

it in the back of his mental closet, where no
one will see, least of all himself. Alan sends
his last e-mails of the day, switches off the
computer, and escapes himself at five
o'clock once again.

*

Ugly Epiphany

Minutes feel like hours as adults hurry by
ignoring her. Just another day outside the
assistant principal's office waiting to be
lectured and Jenny just wants out of it. For a
while, for a long while, she enjoyed school.
Placed in the advanced classes she excelled,
making her parents proud, and making her
feel like she had found her place. She was
stupid, she tells herself, to think her life
could be any different from her mom and
dad's.
It began with an overdue library book. She
was called in to the office, apologized
profusely, and listened while the
condescending little schmuck on the other
side of the desk compared her mistake to
theft. She got two days detention, no big
deal, except she had never been in trouble
before. Then came being a minute late to

27

homeroom. The fact that her car stalled out did not matter to them, rules are rules and this goes on your permanent record. "How do you think an employer will react to your being late?" He asked her as if she did not already work to help make ends meet.
One incident became two, become a dozen, and then more. She has come to realize that it does not matter how bright she is. She plays by all the important rules, which cannot be said of her "peers" that never get in trouble, but all those little rules, those they will leave her out to dry for. Jenny is a smart girl. She knows why. She comes from the wrong kind of family in a small town. Sometimes she thinks of begging mom and dad to move back to the city, but they will not. They think life is better in the 'burbs. She knows better though. Jenny knows it is only better if you are the right kind of person, and she is not. She is convinced that life cannot get better, that the world is full of petty little tyrants like the assistant principal. She cannot know she is both right and wrong, cut off as she is from the wider world. It is also full of people who will see her potential, if she does not give into that growing urge to give up and give in.

*

Saying Hello to Goodbye

Hour stretches into hour, mile into mile, and
Jordan finds himself unable to sleep as he
rests his head against the bus' window. He
would have flown home, but he hates air
travel. It is not that he is afraid of flying, but
the busy, rude, loud commuters and agents
are more than his mild social anxiety
disorder can bear. The bus, crowded as it is,
is easier. A few minutes of shuffling before
boarding and you can drift off once you are
in your seat. At least, that is the theory.
The last time he went home was bad. He and
his pop got into the same old argument, and
it ended with Jordan saying some things he
now very much regretted. A tumor, mom
told him over the phone, in Pop's head
pushing hard against a bunch of blood
vessels. No one knew it was there until it
was too late. Now Pop has a week, maybe
two. He has been told that his father is on
some pretty strong pain medication, and
often does not even recognize his mother.
He wants to say he is sorry, but will Pop
even know? Will it matter?
Choking on his emotions he refuses to cry

here on this bus in the middle of fly-over country. He has learned to hide himself from the public eye, especially in places like this. Funny that it has never been one of the struggles between him and his father. As angry as he can get with his Pop, he still remembers warmly the day his dad socked a coworker for calling Jordan a pansy. Obviously dad loves him, and he loves his dad, so why do they always fight, why is it only now that Jordan appreciates how his dad has always been there for him?

Such silly little differences: Pop does not understand that Jordan does not care about having a house of his own, or this car or that. For his part Jordan never understood, until now, that those "stupid material concerns" were not what his father cared about. He wanted to make sure Jordan was safe, and secure; so many trivial misunderstandings; miles apart and still right there.

Unable to sleep, Jordan pulls out the copy of Don Quixote Pop bought him for graduation. He smiles, just a little, at the poetry of it.

*

That Last, Loose Rock

Six months left Joe tells himself. Half a year
and he can retire. No more uniform, no more
worries, no more headaches, just a life of
relative luxury after a career of service. He
looks across the desk at the fresh-faced,
worried Private First Class, and nearly two
decades of loyalty, honor, and a few
mistakes flash before his eyes. "Why now,"
he asks himself and, beneath his breath, the
young enlisted man. He has come so close,
why this last hurdle before the home stretch?

The kid is not an idealist, not like Joe was
all those years ago. He's not like that boy all
over the news and social media. He was just
caught in an awkward place. He did the right
thing, went to his First Sergeant when he
saw what he accidentally taped at his little
sister's birthday bash. He saw those young
officers take the waitress in back on the
video, he saw what she looked like after, and
did what he was supposed to do: followed
the chain of command. Top, however,
wanted nothing to do with it, and the boys
CC berated him. He knew what he saw,
though, and more to the point why his
commander tried to sweep it under the rug,

31

so he did one more good thing, and brought it to Joe.

"Why me?" The middle-aged officer, bright silver eagle on his shoulder, shakes his head and asks," why not just a little while longer." No, it was not to be, the buck has been passed to him by weaker men, and he does not know if he has the strength. One of the young officers is a Senator's son. They will drag his name through the mud if he helps this naive, honest boy do the right thing. His mistakes, the ones Courtney long ago forgave him for, will be brought out for public consumption, tossed over his unknowing children and parents, burning them as it did him and Court all those years ago. Six more months, and he would have been free.

He sighs heavily. Five administrations he has usually done the right thing, no matter how difficult. He will be true to his oath one more time, the oath to his Commander-in-Chief, God, and the uniform. He smiles wearily at the boy, and picks up the phone.

*

Uncle Vince Comes Home

Henry is happy today. It usually is not the case when mommy and daddy bring him to the big picnics. His cousins are different from him, or more important, he is different from them. The boys like to squish and break the bugs they find and Henry just likes to watch them do their thing. He even knows most of their names, even though he is only eight years old, and can tell the difference between bugs that look a lot a like. He likes bugs, and likes reading about them. He does that a lot because Uncle Vince buys him books filled with all sorts of fun things to learn about bugs, and fish, and birds. He takes Henry to the museum where he works and teaches him anything Henry will learn. That is why Henry is happy. Uncle Vince came to this picnic. He usually doesn't. He came today though, and they talk about all the bugs in the big back yard. Henry asks him why Uncle Frank isn't here and Uncle Vince just tells him he was busy. Uncle Vince is lying, Henry can tell. Grown ups think kids can never tell, but they always can. Just like he can tell mommy and Aunt Vivian are angry with each other. He isn't used to seeing Uncle Vince like this.

Whenever they go to visit him he and Uncle
Frank are always happy and they and
mommy and daddy laugh all night long.
Something is different today. Uncle Vince is
happy, but a little sad too, and Henry just
wants to make him happy, so he keeps
showing him all the things he has discovered
this summer in the yard. He hears some of
his cousins call Uncle Vince words mommy
has told him are bad words. They don't say it
loud, just enough to be heard. Daddy scowls
at them and they walk away, muttering
words Henry doesn't understand and daddy
looks at them the way he looks at the rude
lady who always gets their order wrong at
Burger Boy.

Henry just wants to make it all better. So he
does what he knows makes Uncle Vince
happy. He shows him how much he has
learned, and makes sure and uses all the big
words right. Uncle Vince smiles and Henry
knows everything will be alright.

*

No Shame in Her Game

Maggie leans against the slightly dirty brick
wall. These smoke breaks are a little slice of

heaven for her. They are only a minute or two long, but they are all she gets. She knows she is supposed to get more, but there is too much work to be done. There are too many customers with hungry mouths to feed. There is no time for real breaks, but that is fine, because the money is almost worth it. The money is almost worth missing hours of study time. It is worth losing a half a point on her GPA. A two point seven can still get her into grad school, she tells herself, and she ignores that little voice reminding her that it would be an uphill fight. She needs to work, because otherwise she will graduate up to her eyeballs in debt. There is no shame in this. It is how mom got her to college in the first place. She is being an honest, hard-working American, just like her grandparents. It is not that she does not believe in scholarships, or grants. They are fine, for some people. She wants to hold her head up high though. She wants to say she did it on her own, pulled herself up by her own bootstraps. In the end, she knows she will be better for it.

What is the worst that could happen? There are worse fates than not going to grad school. She will still have her bachelors, probably, and that will be enough, maybe. Even if it is

not, mom has spent thirty years doing
exactly this. Her life is not some horror
show, even if she did give up her dreams.
Mom is hard-working, like a good American
should be. Maggie can and will be the same.
The American dream does come true, she
tells herself, if you just keep your head
down and keep pushing on.
She takes one last drag of her cigarette
before going back inside. A guest has spilled
coffee and no one cleaned it up while she
was gone. It has run down the counter, and
into her book bag. The paper she printed off
before work is soaked. She will have to stop
by the computer lab to print it off again.
Hopefully it will not make her late to class.
Hopefully she can still pass.

*

On The Inside Looking In

Mary sits quietly and alone at her table in
the pavilion. She watches as youngsters run
around Riverside Park, as her son socializes
with his sons and sons-in-law, as her
granddaughter, aided by her friends, sister,
and sister-law makes all the preparations.
She does not offer to help. She long ago got

bored with "thanks mom, but we got this."
So she just sits, and watches, as her family
gathers to celebrate the high school
graduation of her eldest great-grandson,
Peter.

Time was such events were held in her big
back yard, but when Willy passed William
Junior helped her sell the house, using the
money to pay for her nurse. He paid for the
addition to his home so she could live with
him and his Nancy. They have been so very
kind, and Nancy even suggests paying for
the nurse out of their own pocket so her
money can go to the Sisters like Mary
always hoped. The Sisters were so helpful
when they first came here.

Now no one has time for her. They all take
just a few seconds for the obligatory kiss on
the forehead and "you look lovely today
Nana Mary." She understands. They have
their friends, cousins, uncles, aunts, and so
many others to play with. Even little Brynn,
Peter's sister, who normally sits with her for
hours begging her to share tales of what it
was like growing up in the middle of The
Blitz is too busy trying to get the attention of
Peter's best friend's brother. It is as it should
be.

She appreciates her place in the family now.

It hurts sometimes. She misses Willy so much, and the friends they made when they first moved to America after the war. The last of her generation, Mary has no one who understands the importance of all those stories she tells Brynn, not really. Rapt attention and curiosity are nice, but the quiet, solemn nods reminded her she was not alone. Really, though, she is not. She smiles as wide as her nearly ninety year old mouth will allow. Looking out over the generations after her, watching them take so many of the steps she did, seeing the pride in her granddaughter's eyes, the eagerness mixed with anxiety in her son's, Mary realizes that she and Willy made this together, and in a way, he is always here.

*

Porch Swing

Zachary eases back in the big swing on his big porch in his "rundown" neighborhood. People have come and gone over the years. The past few it has mostly been gone. He remembers when his mom and dad brought him up from Birmingham all those years ago to buy this house. It took every last nickel they had ever earned and they both worked like dogs to keep it. He just sits back, a big glass of ice tea in one hand and his pipe in the other.

Little Nellie, his youngest, and her children bug him that he should stop smoking. They nag him that it is bad for him, and that his cough will go away if he quits. Why should he care now though? He's seventy-six years old, and he's been smoking for over sixty of those years. He's going to get called home someday anyway, called home to see his Agnes again, and ma and pa, so what does it matter how? He puffs away, feeling a little defiant as he does so, and just watches the neighborhood come alive in the summer sun. He watches girls walk down the street, gossiping like they always have. Some things never change. Other things don't change either. He sees young men walking shirtless, eager to get into a fight. He never understood that. Anyone can hurt someone; it takes a lot more work to heal. He thinks of Zach Junior. How he used to be like these young men. He thinks of his son working hard to get out from under the trouble he got into, and how proud he is that his boy is a healer now, even if he joins in his little sister's lectures. Zachary smiles wide and

even laughs a little as the firemen open the
hydrant to cool off all the kids.

It's not the same neighborhood he moved
into all those years ago. Still, there are signs,
remnants, and reminders that some things
never change. The kids still play, the moms
and dads still worry, and sometimes, just
sometimes, you get a day with no troubles.

*

Fish Tank

This is Dale's favorite part of the deal: the
party afterward. It is not just the libations,
music, and women in their best little, black
dresses that he appreciates, no, all that is
icing on the cake. He loves that all this
celebration is happening because of him. He
made this, and so many other negotiations in
the past, work, and he gets to stand out of
the crowd, beaming like the proverbial kid
in a candy shop.

He knows, of course, that he did not do it
alone. He makes sure everyone knows he
appreciates the little people, the eager little
worker bees that run around, setting his
appointments and grabbing the hard files
when he needs them. His conversations

always make a point to turn, very briefly, to those who made the deal that much easier for him, in both companies, of course. They smile and laugh at his jokes and tell him what a great boss he is.

His boss pats him on the back as he shakes the other guy's boss's hand. It is never too late or too early to network. Dale does this with gusto. He never spends too much or too little time with any gathered group. He listens intently so he knows everything he needs to know about them. That is important, because you never know when you may be negotiating, or fighting, with them later. You never know what useful little tidbit might help you out later. Everyone is your best friend and your worst enemy.

Men get a hearty pat on the back and women a gentle, not too intrusive, hand at the small of their back. You have to let them know how strong you are. They can smell weakness, and if you show any, you are as good as done. Dale will never let that happen.

No, he works the crowd slow but sure. He makes new contacts, new allies, and meets prospective new employers. Blind loyalty is a sign of weakness. He does all this and basks in his latest success, confident that the

small fry in the pond can never take this
shark.

*

Other Side of the Glass

The giant, posh office feels claustrophobic.
Triple the normal occupancy and people
bouncing off each other like balls in a lottery
tumbler, chattering inanities and sipping
champagne, this is not what Kendra signed
on for. Top of her class she wanted to make
a difference, then, unable to pay her loans on
not-for-profit pay, she wanted to at least
show off her skills. Instead she finds herself
needing to play nice in this dog and pony
show. Her years of education mean nothing,
apparently, just how she looks in her little,
black dress, and how sincere she can smile
despite how much she despises the person
she is speaking to.
It is not that she dislikes vapid discussions
of fashion. She enjoys her time with her
girlfriends, decompressing, focusing on
nothing in particular, window shopping and
people watching. That is what the weekend
is for. Work should be for crunching
numbers, reading contracts and figuring out

the best deal for the boss. That is why she hates these things. They turn work into fun and vice versa and she hates blurring those lines.

She hates pretending she enjoys the company of women who make horrible, privileged comments during lunch. She hates being passive-aggressively pressured into dolling up, rather than wear her normal formal business-wear like the men are allowed to. She hates the guy from the other firm who apparently never took a gender studies class and thinks it is OK to put his hands on her like she was some piece of meat to claim. This is not what she hoped for when she left for school at seventeen. It is the best she can do for now. Maybe in a few years she can parlay this into a management position with a charity, political party, or activist group. Until then she has to grin and bear it. She needs to giggle at insipid jokes, pretend she likes champagne, and learn to walk in high heals all while still being able to play tough with the boys in the conference room. She has the skills, she can be a winner, but she is losing site of the prize and as one more guy invades her space; that scares her.

*

The Ostrich

Still the wallflower, Jenny sinks into the
corner of the banquet hall, grateful to be
assigned the table she was. Twenty years
later these people still frighten her. Never
the pretty one, never the clever one, never
the quick, funny or trendy one, she always
melted into the background. It was safer
there. She did not fit in with the jocks, the
drama geeks or nerds, she was just Jenny
and nobody bothered with her. Standing out
meant risk and she saw what could happen if
you could take risks. Risks were, well, risky.
In two decades that has not changed. She
still avoids standing out. She does her job
faithfully and quietly. Her bosses always
appreciate her, but Jenny avoids accolades.
She does just well enough to get her cost of
living raise and maybe a little more, but not
well enough to get promotions too quick, or
be praised as employee of the month. Those
mean attention, and attention is bad.
She married her first love, because it was
safer. He is quiet, like her, and they live
their safe, unremarkable lives in their tiny
house, with their three children. They have

talked about home schooling, but that means losing a job, that means risk, and they hate risk. Their two eldest children are like them: sweet, polite, and unassuming. They all like to play it safe.

All but the youngest: Bethany likes to explore. She likes to meet people and it frightens Jenny so much. Bethany says hi to strangers in the stores. She likes going places that scare her older siblings. She breaks the rules, she takes the stage, she volunteers, and she stands out. Jenny does not know what to do with her.

She looks out over the banquet hall and sees Taylor Matthieson, the valedictorian who later made a name for herself risking her scholarship to protest university policies. She talks a little with Chuck, who spent years on the wrong track and while he regrets the pain he caused also relishes the adventures he had. Then she remembers Zachary Pryor, and how his sense of fun ended in twisted metal and eating through tubes and she wishes Bethany were more like her and her father. She sinks further into the corner, where it is safe.

*

Silver Wear

Joe looks out over the table, proud of the setting, and of the fragrance filling the air. For a minute he wishes he had his uncle Cenzo's talents in the kitchen, but he knows he has inherited enough culinary skill to make it work. Two plates placed across from each other, bowls of pasta and sauce, an expensive bottle of red and two candles. A perfect setting for this perfect night, a night Joe has done his level best to pretend he forgot, and for the perfect woman.

He remembers it like it was yesterday. He had only been working in Cenzo's deli a month after being discharged from the army and in walks this new counter girl: Katie. She had sass and was way too full of herself. How such a tiny woman thought she could give a room full of men attitude was beyond any of them, but she did, and got away with. She was smart, an honors student in her college, and bold, and nothing like Joe's mom. He had always told himself he wanted a marriage like his parents: a dutiful wife waiting for him when he got home from work with dinner on the table. As carefully hidden memories of mother crying in the pantry creep into his thoughts Joe finds himself thanking God for not giving him what he wanted and for Katie making him a better man.

The last twenty-five years have taken their toll. Gravity has been relentless with both of them, despite gym memberships and yoga classes and he makes a little, self-effacing joke how it is not fair that, even so, Katie is more beautiful now than she was that first day behind the counter. Time has chipped away at them, but all that means is that it has gotten rid of all the two never needed and left them what they required to be one. It left them with Cenzo's deli to run when the old man got too sick to do it himself, it left them with seven years of trying to have a child and a bittersweet summer of sending that girl to college. It left them with photo albums full of a life together.

Joe grins as hears the porch door creak. He lights the candles. It's been a good twenty-five, and there is more to come.

*

Flying With Her Feet on the Ground

The work week has been long and tedious and full of frustrations. Nadia does not care

47

about that now. No filing, no deadlines, no
reprimands and certainly no left-handed
compliments squeezed through gritted teeth;
out here she lets it all go. Out on the dance
floor she lets herself forget her obligations.
Out in the clubs she is queen of her own,
little world and no one can dethrone her.
In her best club wear she saunters from bar
to bar. Her hemlines would give her father a
heart attack but that is his problem, not hers,
certainly not now. She smiles at the guys,
and sometimes the girls, who check her out
without leering. She rolls her eyes at the
people who stare. She moves through the
crowds with ease, a part of them but apart
from them. She rules this night and she
knows it, at least for the first hour, maybe
two.

Nadia buys a drink, and is offered two
others. She laughs and flirts and sways to
the music. Aggression takes over by the fifth
mixed drink and her head feels like it is full
of helium. She likes this part best: the loss of
control and the denial of responsibility. Her
life is full of responsibility, but never on a
Friday night. She lets the bass and the buzz
direct her, letting men touch as much as they,
and she, like, and not worrying at all what
her friends, aunts, sisters or mother would

think.

A little more than half way through the night it catches up with her and ends up in a mess on the pavement outside the last stop on her club crawl. She wipes her mouth and accepts a breath mint from a new friend, straightens herself out and moves on to the next party.

Nadia is out of control and loving it. This is her gift to herself, and to anyone who wants to have a little fun with her.

She won't regret it in the morning. She has taught herself well on that. The only thing she may regret is not having enough water to stave off that hangover. No, Fridays are for no regrets. She lets loose, forgets her chains and for an hour or six, she flies with her feet on the ground.

*

Continuing Adventures

The tiny hand grips his finger as tight as it can and Robert cannot recall ever being so afraid. This little creature in his arms terrifies him more than any challenge he has ever undertaken. For ten years he and Lynn tried so hard to be parents. They knew, right out of grad school that they wanted a family.

For a decade they dealt with the heartache of fertility clinics, special diets, and other seemingly hopeless regimens until finally it happened.

Now that she is here Robert does not know what to make of little Celia Rose. She is tiny, soft, and fragile and her father is so worried he does not have what it takes to prepare her for a cold, harsh and often cruel world.

"What if I fail" keeps sneaking into his thoughts as do the myriad consequences for this brand new human being he cradles. His mind tells him that he and Lynn have made a terrible mistake. He thinks of their college friends who have children starting middle school, and how so many of them seem so unhappy.

Then he remembers his first bike ride and the look on his father's face. He remembers his mother beaming at his first recital. He recalls the happy tears on both of their faces when he walked across that stage to accept his diploma. Robert thinks about his brother-in-law and the love in his eyes when he plays with his children. He looks down at the wrinkled, little face peeking out from her bundle and for a moment the doubts melt away.

Robert knows they are not gone. He and

Lynn have guaranteed themselves two
decades or more of worrying. They may fail,
but then again, they may not. He has no idea
what the future holds for him, Lynn, or little
Celia Rose, and he knows he can never
dispel this fear. He does understand, though,
that if he wants to smile at her first bike ride,
to cry at her first recital, that he owes his
daughter the courage to get past those fears.
He kisses her forehead, promising to find
that courage, and to give her the best life he
can.

*

Proper Support

Simone steps back behind her cash register
in the grocery store. The break was too short,
and the lines are too long, but what else is
she going to do? Her two youngest are still
in high school and their fathers think child
support is just a suggestion and not an
obligation. Why shouldn't they? That's how
the court acts. The last time she got a
payment from Jimmy was thirty-five dollars
five months ago. At least she was able to
buy some school supplies for the kids,
because the school sure as hell doesn't

provide them.

She pushes it all down as far as she can, not thinking about it too much so she can smile for the customers. Mustn't let them know you are a human being with pain and worries just like them. Mustn't let them see the hurt that shoots up your legs and back from arches that fell somewhere between your first and second child. They may not like that, and you wouldn't want to make their shopping experience anything less than stellar.

Simone isn't bitter, not really. She could have it so much worse and she knows it. Two jobs may be a hassle, but they let her rent a slightly run-down house in a small town rather than end up in a complete shit pit of a tenement in the city. It keeps her in a district where maybe her kids have half a chance, though not being from the right family sometimes costs them dearly.

 Besides Devon, her oldest, helps by sending some of his Army check home.

The hours drag by in a dull haze and after a while Simone forgets about her aching feet. There's just no time to think about them. She will remember later, at the end of her shift. Her ankles, knees, and toes will remind her that she is not young and thin like the kids

she works with. They will scream bloody
murder until she pours her G+T (and at one
a night, if you want to judge her you can get
bent) and uses it to wash down some
ibuprofen.

For now she just plugs away. What else is
there to do? There are bills to pay and
mouths to feed. So all she can do is stay on
her feet that little bit longer, and pray they
hold out.

*

Woulda, Shoulda

Other students part like the Red Sea as he
walks down the hall. Adam is used to people
acting weird around him. Ever since he
came back from the hospital no one knows
how to react to him. He wants to tell them
he is still the same guy they went to grade
school and middle school with but he knows
they won't be able to believe him. At the
very least they won't be able to process it.
Just a little accident, a tiny head injury and
everything changes. He walks and talks
different, his nerves won't let him do
otherwise, but beneath it all he still knows,
still feels, the same, but he cannot show
them that, not in any way that will convince
them. None of them see the Jeff that was

always there and still is.

They don't see the funny, smart guy that laughed at all the same jokes, danced to all the same music, and loved all the same movies they did. They only notice the sad, strange person who sometimes needs help opening his locker, who takes longer to answer questions, and has to stay in classes for "special needs" students despite being on the easy track to valedictorian before "it" happened.

All it took was a few bad decisions, really nothing different from what most teens do, but now his life has been turned on its head. He still has a future, but it is tarnished. The accolades that could, and still may, be heaped upon him will be amended with "despite ofs" and "even thoughs." They don't take away the accomplishment, but, yes, they do. No matter how much he wishes otherwise.

He is a reminder. He let's them know how fragile they are and if there is anything a teenager hates, it is someone making them remember they are mortal. One bad choice, one night of fun, and Jeff's hopes and dreams are in doubt, if just a little, and no one, no matter how much they say differently, will ever let forget it. His body, his family, his teachers and his friends, are sirens, announcements, reminding him, and everyone else, that actions have consequences, and he knows that he is a walking, talking, breathing cautionary tale.

*

In Vino

The night begins quietly enough. Helen has one glass, then a second, to celebrate her impending early retirement. She is surrounded by co-workers whom she has known for almost thirty years, people who never really knew the staid and steady school teacher. She and her husband would come to the odd social function, but for the most part kept away save for a small circle of his high school buddies. No one is used to encountering such a chatty version of this unassuming woman, and no one is quite sure what to make of it.

A second glass turns to a third, then a fourth, and by the time she has finished her sixth glass of Pinot Grigio Helen is quite prepared to tell everyone what she thinks of them. Their work ethics could all be better, few of them put the time into the kids, and the younger teachers are obviously in it because they thought it would be easy work, though she lauds those who stuck it out when they learned otherwise. She makes none to veiled suggestions about the Vice Principal and the boys' Gym Teacher, and though everyone assumed to begin with, all are made uncomfortable, even more so than the pair in question, when forced to acknowledge it. For three decades Helen has bottled up her disapproval and tonight that bottle has been uncorked, along with the Riesling and the Shiraz. Her normally perfect diction slumps and she slides sloppily from word to word, though her meaning is perfectly clear. She lets loose a torrent of opinion, and while much of it is giddy, if incoherent, praise, most will only remember being dashed on the rocks of her wit. Their flaws laid bare by someone who has been forced to silently watch them stumble through life while somehow still landing on their feet causes them to shrink slowly away. They want to enjoy sending her off, but instead she is sending them away.

So be it, she thinks in a wine soaked stupor. They have never really been her friends. They sought her approval for all these years, and gave their subdued praise for her efforts. They claimed how much they wanted to live by her example, all while rushing out the door before four. In the morning she may

56

regret it, but for now, she will enjoy finally being able to tell the truth.

*

No More Blaming Luck

Everyone is here. The entire village has shown up for the game, so many people that the new bleachers they built with that extra half million in federal funds is not enough so people crowd around the track where they can. All eyes are on Teddy as he walks to the middle of the field for the coin toss. This is what he has trained for since the first day of Vince Lombardi football all those years ago, and tonight is his night to shine.

He didn't want it to happen quite like this. Brandon is his friend, even if right now he does not realize it. This is the game that will put them in the championship or end both of their high school careers, and with all the local TV stations watching, it could get the winning quarterback into a Division One school. It should be Brandon out here, but he was the one that had to punch that stupid, little stoner right in the mouth in front of a teacher. So of course they had to suspend him, which put Teddy in the limelight.

He feels bad, just a little, but he also knows he is the better player to begin with.

Brandon is good, but being the coach's son was what got him the number one spot, even though Teddy deserved it, and they both know it. At least that is what Teddy tells himself. What their friends tell him now, what his dad has been grumbling about the last three years. He has had few chances to show what he has, and every time he has come through, only to have it dismissed as "garbage time" touchdowns.

Well he is better than that and he will win tonight. No one will be able to deny his talent after this game and he will be able to go to Ohio State, USC, or at least the University of Montana. His dreams can come true and he won't be denied them anymore just because he wasn't lucky enough to have a coach for a dad. He gets to the middle of the field, everyone watching. The ref asks for the call, and Teddy says tails. It comes up heads.

*

Painted In Dark Blue

Long, boring hours sitting in the cruiser have put a cramp in Vic's neck. He twists his head around and puts his arms behind his back before settling back in. This is most nights for him, laying in wait in the same spot, keeping a lookout for people stupid enough to think that breaking the rules "just once" is no big deal, because that "just once" couldn't possibly result in someone's kid going through a windshield, maybe their own. So he spends an hour or more around the bend in the old country road, confident it is just a matter of time.

Then again, maybe confident isn't the right word. It's not like he wants to write someone a ticket. The way people react you'd think they believe he enjoys it. Yes, it's true, he and his brothers in blue have quotas. It would be nice if there were a better tool to measure their performance, he's even suggested a few, but the easiest path wins, and quotas are it. Besides, it's not like the people he tickets are being persecuted. You speed, drive recklessly, or in an unsafe vehicle and you are putting lives in danger. He is trying to protect them, but all they see is the uniform and the badge.

They don't see the dad that takes his
daughter to dance lessons. They don't know
he helped raise his brother and sister
because their dad bailed. They never ask if
he ever wanted to be anything other than a
cop. Sure, in Vic's case he always knew, but
so many of his fellow officers wanted to be
doctors, lawyers, shrinks, and even artists.
They just ended up in the cruiser because it
is where life brought them, for any number
of reasons. They are people, not their job,
but you'd never know that the way folks act.
He doesn't let it bother him too often though.
He knows what he does is important. It may
aggravate the civilians that there are rules
and people there to enforce them, but they'd
be a lot more aggravated without them. He
rubs the cramps out of his thighs just before
the radar goes nuts and the pick up flies
down the road. One more time he flips on
his lights, and hopes it's just another fool.

*

The Forgetting Princess

The aisles are spilling over with costumes of
every variety. They pass witches, nurses,
girl doctors, faeries, amazons, jungle girls

and firefighters. As usual Melanie stops at the princesses. Her mom gives her a look, imploring her to choose something else. She has no grand, cultural agenda that opposes her daughter being a princess. While she counts herself as a feminist she also tells herself that she is not one of "those" kind. Her concern is for her daughter's emotional health.

Melanie is a princess, for the fourth straight year, because she was always daddy's little princess. It was sweet, and still is a little, but her mom worries that she is being obsessive. Her husband is in a far off land, a country she cannot pronounce, because that is where the Marines have sent him, three straight times now. Melanie only knows her daddy's face because they have the internet. She gets to talk to him every week, and every week he reminds her she is his princess. Mom wants to tell him to come up with something else, to tell their daughter she can be anything she wants, but she knows it is important for his sense of continuity.

So Melanie is a princess, again, because that is what daddy wants and she loves her daddy so much, even though she cannot remember what he really sounds like, or smells like, or feels like. She does not remember his favorite food, his favorite music, his favorite movies. She sort of recalls what it felt like when she had a nightmare and daddy came running to her room to pick her up, but even that is fading a little every day. She forgets how it felt to see him smile at her, or how bad she felt when he was angry with her. She no longer knows what it was like to see him waiting for her when she got out of kindergarten for the day.

She remembers that she is his princess though, and she holds on to that as tight as she can. It is all that Melanie has left of her daddy, until he comes home, and she will be a princess every Halloween and every day if she can. She will have her daddy back in that small way, for that short time, and it will have to be good enough.

*

The Next Turn

Luis does not get it. He sits in the passenger side seat, his son, Roberto behind the wheel and he does not understand. Over and over people tell him this is a bittersweet moment; teaching his boy how to drive means accepting that he is a growing young man almost ready to go out into the word on his own. They tell him she should be proud of his son, and he is, but they also tell him that he should be sad that soon he will be leaving the nest. To him that makes no sense whatsoever.

For sixteen years Luis has fed, sheltered and clothed Roberto, with help from his wife Shelly, of course. They have provided for their son in every conceivable way. They have dealt with the worry of his first sleep over, and enjoyed the pride of watching him bat in the game winning run. They have done everything a parent is supposed to, and now, as his only child drives for the first time, Luis thinks about how happy he will be in a handful of years when that child leaves the shelter of their home.

It is not exhaustion or unhappiness with being a parent that drives these thoughts. Roberto has always been a good boy and Luis and Shelly could not be happier with him. They have loved every minute of being parents, even the hair-raising ones. Instead it is the oncoming sense of accomplishment that he looks forward to. Why would anyone dread the idea of their child becoming a fully developed adult? Isn't that the point of being a father or mother: to prepare the next generation to be ready to take on the responsibility of living on their own?

Luis looks forward to that day, whether it is in two years when his boy graduates high school or in six when he graduates from college (with honors, of course.) He relishes the certainty that he has given Roberto opportunities that he and Shelly never had, and that his son is a good enough man to take advantage of and appreciate them. For now though he simply enjoys the pride he is feeling now, as they take their time in the abandoned parking lot before he tells him to head out to the street.

*

Failing Shields

The bright lights in the laundromat make it easier to see the stains on your clothes. They also make it harder, Matt thinks, to hide. He wants to bury his face in his book, to not be noticed by anyone. He especially does not want to be noticed by her. He does not want her to realize that he has seen her, that he has been fighting his insecurities, heaped for decades upon him by a disappointed mother and weak father, to work up the nerve just to say hi.

He first saw her, or at least first took notice of her, in their intro to philosophy course. She was brilliant, speaking up every chance she got, challenging the professor and other students. She was brave, energetic, and genius. Everything Matt wishes he could be but is painfully aware he is not. Her eyes a pale blue that he could lose himself in if he had the nerve to look into them the handful of times they spoke. When they sit waiting for the classroom to open she says such kind things to him, and admonishes him to lift his head when he walks. "If you are looking at the floor, how can you see where you are going?"

"I'm not going anywhere," is his knee-jerk response that he swallows down, lest she see just how really pathetic he is. He wants her to want him, but knows it is impossible. It's not that he buys that "nice guy/jerk" crap his gamer buddies always go on about. Matt knows he is a loser and doesn't deserve someone awesome, cool, and nice like her. He is awkward and always afraid. He cries at the drop of a hat and knows he is a bit of a sissy. Why would anyone ever want to be with him? No, better not to even pretend she, or anyone, would ever be more than a good friend, which for Matt is good enough, he supposes, as much as just once he would like to be kissed.

So he hides as best he can behind his copy of Sword of Shannara. He buries himself in his chair, sinking lower so she cannot see him. He's saving them both the hassle, he thinks to himself. He does not see her walk up, smiling nervously "hey, that's my favorite book."

*

Meta Below

The odor of stale candy and dried soda fills Pete's nostrils and he sags against his cart as he pushes it through the multiplex halls. He grunts while bending over to scrape up the ground-in gum in the carpet. It will have to freeze off and will take him forever and he barely cares at this point, wanting only to get through the banality of his shift so he can go home and crack open a cheep beer. The dull ache in his soul has been replaced with a mildly angry resignation that this is his place, and all he will ever have.

It was not always like this. Fresh out of college, with a four point oh in theater, he was going to set the stage on fire, probably metaphorically, as he produced play after brilliant play. He was going to redefine drama and open the minds of actors and theater goers alike. They would heap mountains of praise on him and he would retire, early of course, to reviews and retrospectives claiming him to be the greatest of legends. That was seven years ago, when he came to the city to make his mark. Instead the city marked him.

He has not completely given up. He still reads the dailies. He keeps in the know, but he has accepted that for real people, unlike the characters in a play, dreams often do not come true. Some small part, deep inside, hates himself for being so willing to acknowledge his fate. His fire has been doused by the cold rains of life and he cannot reignite it no matter what, even enough to try a new career at the entry-level. Cleaning up after vapid movie goers only compounds his ennui and hopelessness. This is a dull, uninspired life, he tells himself. He lets his heart and mind sink ever deeper into a groove of routine of self-pity and loathing. This life is one of boredom and monotony, unworthy of anyone's interest. Who would care what a failed producer/play-write

turned janitor does with his life? Who would
pay to watch or read about that? He does not
know it yet, but way back in the recesses of
his once blazing mind, a spark has lit the
kindling.

*

Riding Home

Raw nerves keep her hands shaking.
Breathing has become increasingly difficult
the entire ride from Binghamton to
Jamestown. Kate knows she is doing the
right thing, that it should have been done so
many years ago, at least some time in the
year and a half she and Debbie have been
together. She called her mom and told her
they needed to have a talk. "Have you met
someone?" Mom asked, knowing she and
Deb have lived together for six months. She
is either the queen of delusion or truly does
not have a clue and Kate's stomach twists
for blaming her mom for something she
should have dealt with.
She does not have it as hard as some, she
knows, but Kate also knows, from her
upbringing, from dozens of arguments over
politics, and from long, uncomfortable

silences at Thanksgiving that she also has it so much harder than many today. Deb's mom cried tears of joy when she was told that they were moving in together. They aren't engaged but Sandy drops hints like Chernobyl potatoes, always eager to plan an over the top wedding for them. Kate has fought past her resentment. If she hadn't she and Debbie would not still be together. It sits in sharp contrast though to what awaits them at the other end of the Southern Tier Expressway.

The gas station coffee comes back up on her a bit as they finish the last few miles through the mountains, almost home. She sees Deb shoot her a worried look; Deb, her super hero who stands up to everything and everyone, unafraid because she knows the consequences of stepping down. She wishes she was as brave. Kate knows she cannot lean on her for this. No, the next part is all on her, and the only thing her girlfriend (they both hate the word "partner," it's not like they own a bake shop together) can do is be there with a shoulder to cry on if it comes out for the worst.

They pull up the gravel drive way as Mom watches. Deb puts her hand on her shoulder gently and smiles as she opens the door.

Somehow seeing the Reverend standing there makes it easier. She is less an idea and more a person. Kate takes a deep breath and her chest loosens. "Hi mom."

*

Always On

Kayla gets through about half her bills before it hits her. Sitting with the pile of papers with the bright sunlight pouring into her kitchen it becomes too easy to let her mind drift. The sunbeam hits that dreadful stack and pulls her mind away and she drifts into dreams of another life, one in which she followed her ambitions across country to become a star, or just left town to try to make it another way in another place. She sighs and smiles and all the things that might have been dance about her head.
It's not that she is unhappy. Quite the contrary, Kayla is very happy. She has a wonderful husband four amazing kids and a small business of her own. She keeps busy with the house, projects and volunteering. She loves every minute and really would not

change it for anything. It is just that
sometimes these moments come to her and it
is pleasant to think about what might have
been.

She has always been like this, and when she
was younger her mother hounded her for it.
"You gotta get your head out of the clouds
Kayla." She would tell her and for a while it
would bring her back. Kayla would put her
nose to the grindstone and pull her grades up,
eventually becoming Salutatorian of her
class and on to graduating college with
honors. After changing majors six times of
course.

Then she met Malik and he did not care that
sometimes, on their dates her eyes would be
focused far away. He would just ask her
what she was looking at. The first four times
she said nothing until the fifth date she told
him. She told him how she could never stop
day dreaming, how her head could just pull
her away. He just smiled that bright smile of
his, telling her he figured, and that was the
reason he was drawn to her.

Malik accepts her for who she is. He
encourages her to dream, to drift, and to
come back again. The latter he does through
just loving her as she is, and Kayla knows
how lucky that makes her in this world. So

for a half hour her mind wanders until it makes its way back to the task at hand, rejuvenated and ready to go.

*

All Apologies

"It's not you, it's me." That was the cliché Lance dropped on Chase when he walked out the door. Three years of marriage he is willing to throw away and the best he can do is hand her that tired line. So now she is left wondering whether she should be angry, sad, or guilty. She asks herself if it really is her. Could she have been more patient? Could she have been more supportive? Should she have been more aware?
All the expected worries march through her thoughts. She wonders about the late hours he spent at the shop with all the college girls that work for him. Doubts about her own appearance sneak into the equation and she examines herself in the mirror. Years of yoga, Pilates, gym memberships, and more have staved off gravity, but not enough. She is old, at thirty-two, and not as pretty as all those women in the shop, no matter what she wears, how much make-up she applies,

and despite the coy glances from the boy at the supermarket. Why wouldn't Lance want someone else?

It is so much easier, for both of them, to make it about that. It is so much simpler to make it about sex and mid-life crisis than to look back at what they both knew, or more importantly did not know. For instance they did not know that getting married because "I am pushing thirty and should have a husband/wife" was not a particularly good idea. They did not know that ignoring all the basic values that were in conflict was asking for unhappiness. They did not ask themselves how well they really knew each other. So now they are here, and rather than looking at the foundations they never really built, they are building a new foundation to create a temple of bitterness.

Because "it's not you, it's me" and suspicions of infidelity are less difficult. It is so hard to say you were wrong, and "I am sorry" even when it is to yourself. There is so much less effort in loathing, of oneself and the other, than to walk through that door to real happiness.

*

The New Navigation

The room is bright and cheerful and completely contrasts with Brandon's mood. The "incident" fills his mind with a sticky, dark fog and part of him does not want to move out of it. The fog is familiar, it is all he has ever known from middle school on and thirty years later it seems impossible to give up now, thought that is exactly why he has come to this place.

Everyone is nice here. They smile calmly and politely answer every question; even the ones Brandon thinks are stupid. They want to help him, and let him know every step of the way. No one minds that he has arrived an hour early, as afraid to be late as he is of everything else. Without his asking a receptionist lets him know the cafeteria is right around the corner. They never mention the "incident," the one with a garden hose, running car, and a closed garage.

The hour ticks away and he thinks about Mindy finding him. Shame fills his heart as he thinks of his daughter coming home from college to do laundry and opening the garage door to the cloud of exhaust. He thinks about the horror that must have been in her eyes, and about the anger and worry he saw in them when he woke up in the hospital. Those eyes followed him, even when she wasn't around, for the two months he stayed there.

Now is the hard part. Now he is out on his own again. Mindy has moved back home but his doctors insisted, and he agreed, that he has to be responsible for his well being. He has to make his appointments and keep them without help if he is going to banish the fog once and for all.

Even now though, with all this knowledge, surrounded by these wonderful people, he is still unsure. The fog has been all he has known, with only brief escapes when he met Ginny, then married her, and when Mindy was born. A life without it will be unfamiliar, but if he is going to have a life, he needs to clear it all away. For the first time in decades, frightened as he is, he can imagine a life without it.

*

One Step, Then The Other

Dylan watches her as she sleeps. She looks so peaceful and he wishes he could capture that peace for her forever. Lying on her side she seems vulnerable but strong at the same time and he does not know what to make of his or her feelings. It is the end of their high school "career" and no one thought they would last this long, and no one expects them to last much longer. He wonders if Jen agrees with them.

This was their first time. They waited as long as they could bear. Each wanted it for so long, but they wanted it to be perfect. Prom did not seem right and after graduation seemed too far away, at two weeks. So they decided to make a special date night, driving to his dad's cottage after dinner and a movie. It was awkward, exhilarating, a little frightening, and a lot quicker than he would have thought. He tried not to call attention, and Jen seemed to enjoy herself, but how could he know? When they were done he leaned in and told her he loved her and she just said "oh."

"Oh," as if he had set them on a track she was not sure she wanted to be on. Like a kid who was told to do a chore that they did not hate, but really did not want to do. Dylan had no idea what to make of that. Did she want to break up? Were they ever really in love? Maybe she just wanted a clean break, what with their schools being an eight-hour drive apart. It kind of made sense, but he desperately wanted to make it otherwise.

Sitting in the dark room, watching the moonlight dance over her, he is not sure he can let go. She has been the only woman he ever loved, though everyone tells him there is a big world full of people to meet. She shifts restlessly to her back and he grins as he pulls her hair out of her mouth. He kisses her on her forehead gently and buries his face into her shoulder. Maybe this is it, but if it is, he is going to let himself enjoy it, basking in her glow, as long as he can.

*

Neither Or

Jan waits for her friends at the loud new pub with all the TV screens. There is little in the way of lighting but the flat screen, HD televisions keep the room fairly bright. She sips away at her rum and coke and eats pistachios, enjoying the few moments to herself that her office-less job and child free life allow her. She politely turns away the attention of younger men attempting to win the cougar over. It is flattering, in a way, she supposes but it gets oh so tiresome after a while.

"You just have to meet the right guy." family tells her. Some insist that maybe it is just the right woman, which perfectly cool with them of course. Jan always just shrugs her shoulders. She does not want that, any of it. She is happy on her own and really does not feel the need for physical contact. Learning to grin and bear it as everyone suggests she just is not doing it right, or should see a doctor is a chore this happily single woman has turned into an automatic response. Apparently there is something wrong with being happy on your own, and with not needing the touch of another.

She has heard in the last few months that there are others like her, and that some of the queer community has embraced asexuals as part of their community. Being a cause, however, is not her thing. "Why can't I be me," she asks more often "without anyone turning it into some kind of big deal?" All Jan wants is to earn her keep, make enough for her townhouse and car, and enjoy whatever else the world has to offer: camping, arts, sports, and everything else that is not having a family or sex. What is so weird about that?

Her friends arrive after a little longer and
have brought a new member of the group.
The pretty femme smiles at her and Jan
suppresses the urge to roll her eyes. Another
set up, and another let down for the others.
She wishes they would just stop. She wishes
it could be no big deal.

*

Repeating the Offense

Corey keeps his right hand in his pocket as
he drinks his coffee. He honestly is not
thinking about how that might be a
subconscious move, a desire to keep the
weapon out of sight and out of mind, but if
you were to ask him he would probably
acknowledge you had a good point. He does
not want to think about that hand or what it
did just minutes ago. His shame threatens to
choke him. It nearly frightens him into a
closet where he does not have to admit to
himself what he has done. No, Corey may
not know that he might be hiding his hand
from himself, and his victim, but the sting
reminds him of the truth.
He had always promised that he would
never be like his father. Dad kept five belts

that he never wore hanging in the rec room
closet. You never knew when, where, or
why, but the old man would scowl and point
in the direction of that closet, and Corey and
his brothers knew that they were to go and
pick the instrument of their punishment.
Sometimes, the bad times, he would not
even wait and would take his frustration out
on them with his bare hands. Those were
some of the worst moments of Corey's
childhood, those chaotic moments of fear
and violence that left him bruised though
after a while he learned not to cry because
that just made it worse.

It had been building for a while: a lost
contract here, a flat tire there, and an endless
parade of minor frustrations. Corey had to
be tough though. Do not let it get to you,
only weaklings let it get to them and he
could never tell you why he thought that bit
of advice from a man he hated as much as he
loved was any good. It was just how he was
programmed.

So in a moment of weakness he lashed out at
Mason, over an accidentally deleted e-mail.
It was so quick he did not even have time to
process it until his son was in his room
crying. Corey is not stupid, or selfish, he
will apologize to his boy. He will be

stronger than the old man, and get the help
he needs. His wife says nothing as he passes
her to swallow his pride and save his child.

Remembering To Want

It is unpleasantly warm in the little coffee
shop, still Rebecca remains in a good, but
nervous, mood. She wears a nice, loose, tan
sweater with her favorite long, black skirt
and boots. It is important to look presentable,
but she is conscious of the need to not
overdo it. It has been so long since she has
done this and is a little afraid, but not too
much, of screwing it up.
Ten years, that was the last time she was on
a date. It had never been easy for her.
Rebecca never thought she was as pretty as
her friends, as much as they may have
claimed otherwise. Besides, she was always
had her studies, and then work, to worry
about. Once she was on her own for a bit it
never really made sense to put herself out
there. She was content with her little house
in the burbs and her vacations. She liked
going to the shows she wanted to on her
own terms. There was never a need to check

what the other person wanted to do. It was not that she never had urges, but they just were not important to her.

Now in her mid thirties all of her friends' kids are entering middle school. They regale her with lives full of recitals and track meets. Their joy is apparent and it makes her feel like she is missing out. So she figured it was time to get back up on that horse. That is why she is waiting, trying to forget how much she is sweating, overdressed as she is for the warm cafe.

The guy arrives right on time and he is handsome enough and polite and Rebecca tries to pay attention because he is interesting. Her thoughts, however, wander to that next vacation, the addition she wants to put on the house, and to that book she never wrote. She has all these hopes and dreams that have nothing to do with other people's lives.

She smiles politely at this man, his name is Paul, and decides they can just have some fun. It is OK to live life how you decide. She does not need someone else to complete her, not when there is so much more she wants, and she plans on going after it all.

*

Re-Entry

"You're so brave" they tell Helena her first day back at work. That phrase has been uttered so many times in the last month it almost lacks meaning for her. It is not that she does not appreciate the displays of affection, the reflexive politeness of peers and associates, the genuine concern and love coming from long time friends. She knows they all mean well and some are honestly impressed or caring. She is grateful for them even if her declarations of that gratitude have become somewhat robotic the last few weeks.

Her hair has grown back and she can handle the bus ride without getting winded now. Skin that turned from the healthy bronze of an active woman to a sickly, pale, white-pink has regained some of its color. It has been a long thirty days since her doctor announced she was tumor free, after an even longer two-year battle to make that happen. Two years full of chemo, home health aids, and so many moments of false promise. After all that she had to get back into the game: back to church, back to her charities, back to her family, and back to work. To do less would drive her insane.

That is why she cannot understand why they think she is brave. She is healthy now, why would she not want to reclaim her life? If going after what you want and need, at a pace acceptable to your GP and oncologist, is brave, what does it say of people who face real danger for doing so? It is kind, she knows this, but it makes her feel self-conscious. She does not want to be a survivor, she just wants to be. Helena is no dummy, she understands that weird, little cancer with a name she cannot pronounce will always define her in some way, she just wishes she could escape it, for just a while. She cannot, however, and though it is emotionally tiring, Helena accepts this. She smiles and thanks her co workers when they compliment her. She listens to their somewhat intrusive questions. Then she puts her nose to the grindstone and gets back to it. Maybe she is brave, she lets herself think, if only for being willing to walk this gauntlet of well wishers.

*

Squeaky Ball

Tyler swallows hard before making his way
across the gym floor. He is president of his
middle school student body, on high honor
roll, and captain of his modified football
team, and still he has never been more afraid
in his life. His father raised him right, even
if he had to do it on his own, and Tyler knew
what he had to do when he realized how he
felt about Lori. After the varsity game, at the
dance, Tyler would do what he wanted to
do.

Lori is not a popular girl. She is awkward
and dresses haphazardly. She usually keeps
her head down in the hallway, trying to
avoid eye contact and seeing the other kids
point and whisper. She comes from a broken
home as well, but from the "wrong" side of
town. She and Tyler are worlds apart and yet
they spend an hour a day together as lab
partners for science.

Despite his grades he expected her to treat
him like a stupid jock, but she never did.
She never asks about the big game: why
they won or lost. She never treats him like
he is special or different, and Tyler likes that.
He and Lori finish their assignment early
every time and find other things to work on,

avoiding the uncomfortable silence. Once and a while she even smiles from underneath the red hair that she lets fall in front of her face.

So now he makes his way, lump in his throat, across the basketball court, a symphony of sneakers on wax playing over the DJ's selections. He knows what he is about to do may ruin his reputation in the brutal politics of the eighth grade, but he does not care. "Don't worry what other people think," his dad's words echo in his brain and that advice has always served him well.

He reaches the bleachers where Lori sits silently with her small group of fellow outcasts. No one looks up at him until he reaches out his hand. "Hi," he winces as his voice cracks "you wanna dance?" His chest tightens as she looks up and smiles.

*

Squeaky Wheel

Taylor should be at his middle school dance. That is what fourteen year-old young men are supposed to do. Instead he finds himself outside of a super market in an early November snowstorm. It figures, he thinks to himself, that global warming would take a break the year he is old enough to work a real job. He wants to be at the dance, but instead he is here, because that is what life has handed him.

He wants to be at the dance, but cannot be because momma's two part time jobs do not pay enough and do not leave her enough time to go to DSS. He wants to be showing off on the basketball court with his friends, dancing with all the fine young ladies, but child protective services is OK with him working in this cold, but not with momma leaving them alone to work a third job. He wants to be sneaking behind the bleachers with one of those young ladies, but his brothers and sister need food in their belly so he has to sit in this cold.

The owners of the store, a franchise, provide them with cheap gloves and paper-thin jackets. Taylor has shoveled the walk twice and helped the two people who risked this storm on a Friday night with their groceries. He is out here alone now because Frank, the older guy he works with complained. Frank told Mr. Weicezck it was wrong to have a kid out in this weather. Frank was looking out for him, and Taylor just kept his head down, telling Mr. W it was alright, because he and momma have gotten sick of the way some of the volunteers at the soup kitchen look at them.

Momma hates this, he knows. She wishes she could get a good job. She is smart enough, but she never learned to drive and without the money for lessons, she never will. Not being able to drive means fewer people willing to hire her. It's a vicious circle. So Taylor works instead of having fun, and he pulls good grades at school because he believes momma when she says that is his only ticket out of here. He can't be like Frank, he can't make noise, otherwise he will be in the cold forever, instead of the dance floor.

*

New Storage Room

Tia stands at the end of the hall, paralyzed with more emotions than her thirteen year old mind can process. She stares, intently, at the open door at the end and into the room full of boxes. Toys she will no longer play with, dad's gear from his army days that he keeps for old time's sake, and moms keepsakes she hopes Tia will one day take into a home of her own. They were supposed to be shared. That big "closet" at the end of the hall is not really a storage room.

It is Anthony's room, or at least, it was. Pennants, trophies and collages haphazardly put together with photos of his high school buddies and sweetheart are all packed away in one of those boxes. His bed has been disassembled. Bookshelves are no longer a small library of a young man intent on getting into Princeton, but a home for cardboard containers full of tiny knickknacks. Almost every sign of Tia's big brother has been wiped away.

Mom and dad talked a lot about it. It is a bigger room and they offered it to Tia, it had been months and they thought it was time for the change, but she just could not bring herself to move into it. So after much discussion this is what it has become, just another room. It is like they want him to go away, like they want to forget.

In her heart, Tia knows that is not true. It was just time to move on. Only she was not ready to move on. She wanted to keep his room as a monument to her big brother. She wanted no one to ever forget that he was here, that he was real, and that he was taken too soon for being in the wrong place, in the wrong time, with the wrong color skin, while visiting friends. She does not want him to go away.

In time she will know that this room does not hold Anthony that her memories are where his home is now. In time she will not be stunned by the change. It will hurt less, eventually. Not today though. Today she cries a little more, and just wants things they way they were. Who wouldn't?

*

The Quiet Explosion

He is shaking. Russel has just realized this. Tears running down his cheek and he cannot stop his hands from trembling. Big Russ, the toughest guy anyone knows and he is sitting here in the bright lights of the emergency room crying like a baby. He got the call an hour ago and almost got into an accident speeding here, his heart is ready to burst as conflicting emotions explode out of him. "Your son has been in a car crash." They told him and he felt all the blood drain from his face. Russ is a fireman and he knows what a wreck looks like and the images of

90

his son's fragile flesh tangled with steel and fiberglass forced themselves into his mind. He was ready for the worst when he walked through those doors. The look in the doctor's face was all he needed and suddenly the man everyone else leaned on could not stand up. Then his phone rang again.

"Dad, I'm sorry, I fell asleep on the train, I didn't want to get into the car when we were all drunk. I think I left my wallet at the party." Little Russ was OK. His best friend's boy, a kid who looked a lot like Little Russ picked up the wallet for him. He did not have to bury his boy and he was so relieved he laughed and cried out loud in front of everyone. Then it hit him.

His boy was alive and Jimmy's was not. He was so grateful it was not his own son and hated himself so much for being so happy when the worst thing that could ever happen to a father was happening to his friend. It was as if every emotion he could ever feel hit him all at once. He collapsed into a chair and openly wept. No one stopped him, no one even went near him. The nurses stood back and let him feel it, he needed to. Now he sits there, shaking, and as Little Russ walks into the emergency room Big

Russ charges him, smothering him in his love. His boy is embarrassed, he does not know what has happened yet, and over the kid's shoulder he sees Jimmy walk in. Big Russ recognizes the pale expression and lets his boy go, ready to do the ugly deed for the doctors.

*

Hobby, Habit, or Hazard

Sitting in the home office late at night, the lights off, wife and kids in bed, Jason stares intently at the monitor. He has does not bother to lock the door, the room is on its own at the end of a long hallway and he has closed the blinds. This is his time, his hour or two, or three, with no accounts to review, no bills to pay, no kids to drop off at practice; Just Jason and his "hobby."
He knows no one knows, especially Gwen. He does his own laundry, takes out his own trash and makes it clear when the office door is closed he is not to be disturbed. He tells them he is busy with work and of course they believe him. Twenty different tabs open on his browser and he clicks furiously from one to the next, opening link after link of

young women in all sorts of positions.
His heart races as his hand moves and part
of him worries that someone will disobey
his rules and catch him. It excites him, a
little, to think about that, making his special
time that much more special. His breathing
quickens and his eyes dart from screen to
door and back again and the girls are so
enticing and before long he is finished. At
least, he is finished for the first time tonight.
He goes on like this for who knows how
long, biting his lip and gripping himself tight.
It is raw and nerve-wracking and oh so
much like heaven to Jason and it seems,
these days with all his responsibilities, to be
the only joy he gets in the world. Some
nights, nights like tonight, he is at it until the
break of dawn. "Working late" he will tell
Gwen, and she believes him.
He has to think that. He does not want to
imagine Gwen walking in, or lying in their
bed wondering what he is doing. He cannot
think about her, or the kids, or his neighbors
or anyone else. Just Jason, and his "hobby"
until the morning comes.

*

Fog in the Forecast

Paige sits in the kitchen chair leaning over the back drawing pictures in the foggy windows of her fourth floor apartment. It is big and clean and has all the newest amenities and she is not quite sure what to do with the space. Boxes are stacked in the corners waiting to be unpacked but at the moment all she wants to do is look out the window into the rainy day.

The move was for the best she tells herself: nearly three thousand miles between her mistakes and a new life. She has an excuse now, not to be at her mother's place once a week. She never has to see any of her exes. Every awkward moment is in Southern California and here in Western New York she can start fresh. It will be easy, why wouldn't it be?

The new job helps, of course. Three times the salary she has ever made, great benefits and they even paid for her to move here. She has her own team and a contract that gives her lots of leeway to make the job what she wants it more or less in the time she wants to. Why then, does she feel so uncertain?

She tries to convince herself it is the weather. Rochester is not Los Angeles and she only needs to get used to the cold. Paige is certain that time will fix all that and she can make a new life, new friends and be happy here. That is her mantra, a prayer to banish the nagging doubts about the good things she left with the bad. She will be happy, and she will not feel guilty. Fifteen years of taking care of mom was enough, now it is her sisters' turns.

Looking out over downtown and the Genesee River becomes harder as the rain falls ever faster and obscures her view. The window fogs up even more and she refuses to acknowledge how appropriate that is. She demands certainty from herself and is certain she will get it. Outside, the forecast is less sure.

*

Stain At Home

Gravy dribbles down Harry's chin and on to his well-worn Oakland Raiders tee. He shovels the frozen turkey dinner in, grunting happily as he chews away. His boys are up on San Diego right now which is all he needs to be happy. Candy wrappers surround his decades old recliner in an

otherwise spotless living room and for the
time being it does not bother him.

Eventually it will. Sooner or later his boys
will have a bad call made against them or
lose the game. Worse, the hated Broncos
may win their game and for Harry there's
nothing so unjust. His blissful state will
crumble away and Peg will get the brunt of
it. It's her own fault for not cleaning the
place the way it ought to be. It's like she
forgets that his recliner is part of the living
room. She avoids it and him on Sunday, just
because he gets a little rambunctious.

He's never hit her; at least, he doesn't think
so. That's why he's so confused. It's not like
they couldn't replace the few things he's
broken, well except her mother's china but
why something like that's so important
completely escapes him. He wipes the gravy
from his face with the tee and calls out for
more beer.

Peg gets it to him right away. At least she's
good for that. She never bore him children
and then said maybe the doc was right about
it being something wrong with him. Harry
never hit Peg, but he came real close that
day. How could she shame him like that? In
front of the doctor no less. No, Peg is just
barren and he should have found himself a

woman who could do her duty, but instead
he stays with her because that's what God
intended, not that Harry ever goes to church.
She walks into the living room just as the
Chargers pick up a fumble for a touchdown.
Harry jumps out of the chair screaming
dropping the dinner in the same old spot.
Peg looks down at the floor before turning
back to the kitchen to grab the cleaning
supplies. She tries not to think too much
about the stain.

*

A Little of This

Sidewards glances shoot from all over the
all you can eat buffet and the boys could
care less. A dozen old buddies with a dozen
conversations, each over the other, and none
of them is offended by the constant
interruptions, interjections, and intercessions.
A storm of syllables and laughter rushes in
all directions from their tables and the other
patrons try to be as far away as possible. Not
that even one of the boys notices.
They are too busy catching up and carrying
on. Pictures of children and grandchildren
get passed around, as do stories of

promotions, vacations, celebrations, and the one amputation. Lenny gives the others a hard time, pretending to be hurt about the guys not holding the door for "One Leg Lenny" and then laughs his ass off when Jack fumbles over himself apologizing. They have known each other since they were kids, and have lived through half a dozen wars and even more Presidents. The world is changing around them but they still allow themselves this once a year ritual. This is why they do not concern themselves with the disapproval of the young folk around them. Nothing will put a damper on their mood; even as they take a moment to console Clark on his Gina's passing. Life is too long to not enjoy it to its fullest. It is only a few seconds of relative quiet and then back to their fun.

Back to recalling stories, even if they do not recall them the same. Lenny remembers serenading Jim's little sister, though Jim insists he thought a cat was dying in the alley that night. There is feigned indignation followed by raucous laughter, and an endless barrage of flirting with the hostess. Some of the boys make remarks the others do not like, but they accept, after fifty plus years, that the best of friends do not see things the same way.

After hours of conversation, and plates piling in front of them, the boys slowly get up. Gianni throws a wink in the direction of the hostess giving Jim a chance to remind him that she is probably younger than his great grand-daughter. Another year has passed and while no one says it, they all hope they are all here next year, without letting that dampen being here now.

*

The Trap

Surrounded by luxury, Caitlyn slumps in her big, canopy bed. Everything in her room is white. It is clean, expensive, and made to impress; only the best for the Colemans' only daughter. Trophies fill bookshelves. Awards for tennis, field hockey, volleyball, and swimming sit alongside certificates for finishing various classes in music and dance. Hers is a life of accomplishment and opportunity.

She rules the roost in her upper-middle class suburban high school. Pretty, smart, funny, and always well dressed, Caitlyn is the envy of every other girl there. The pool party is always at her house, always catered thanks to her parents, and always the social event of the week. The other party, the one parents pretend not to know about, is held at the home of Caitlyn's very handsome, very popular boyfriend. He is a sweet enough guy, but they both know in July they will graduate from more than High School.

Her life is so perfect, so easy in so many ways, so why does she feel so lost lately? She wants to hide under her covers today and never come up. She knows part of it is nerves about going on to college. Here at home she is the big fish and she will have to fight to gain a place among the leaders at University. Deep down, though, she knows that is not it.

Caitlyn knows her path has been chosen for her. Her parents have groomed her for success, and she will succeed. She will be the best and brightest in college, just as she was in high school. She will meet the right man, and have her two point five kids and live in the right neighborhood throwing all the best social events. She will chair a charity or three and will look the other way, like mom, when her husband's eyes, hands, and possibly other body parts wander.

Any choice for another life is impossible,

she thinks. No peace corps, teaching in an inner city school, or living with an artist in his tiny studio apartment for her. No real adventure or learning. Just a routine from which there is no escape. Caitlyn looks at the bottle of prescription sleeping pills, and wonders if there is a way out.

*

Taking the Baton

Crisp, October air stings Bill's nostrils a bit even as he sweats under his autumn, outdoor gear. His knee aches some from all the back and forth. The better part of his morning has been piling new firewood into the wheel barrow to take it to be stacked next to the cottage. They will need it in the coming months as another Northeast winter approaches. His shoulders groan, his back cries, and his fingers complain and yet Bill is happy as he works.

The cottage has been in his family for three generations now. Four if you count Bill's kids, who are too young to appreciate it just yet. It is where they hold all their holiday celebrations and the many birthday parties that come in the cold time of year. Decades of happy memories are held in that wood-paneled building and he wants to make sure there are decades more to come, which means making sure everything is taken care of.

In the past those duties fell to his dad or granddad. His grandfather, though, had been wheel chair bound the last few years of his life, and has been gone for two years now. Dad wanted to help this year, but after the heart attack, his doctor said it was not a good idea. So now it falls to Bill.

As much as he misses dad's commanding presence, Bill loves this. It is his turn to make sure everything goes right. It is his responsibility and he will not let the family down. He watches with pride as his boys and his nephews help how they can, raking leaves and cleaning windows. His brother, Ted, is getting the old furnace going for the season. Everyone coming together and looking to Bill to get it organized, while mom and dad relax in the den watching the game.

He is pushing forty, so Bill does not know how long he has to enjoy this before passing the duties on to his boys or his nephews, but he will do the best while he can. As he pushes the wheel barrow through the wet leaves and the scents of autumn fill the air, he is content to know he can keep the traditions going a few more years.

*

Checklist

So much to do, Celia sighs, before Robert Junior gets home. She straightens his room for the thirtieth time. The refrigerator has been stocked, and re-stocked. His favorite shows are once again front and center on the DVD shelf. Four years of her baby being away, except for the odd holiday and she is utterly over the moon. Robert Senior just rolls his eyes as she buzzes about like a bee. He does not understand.

To him, his boy is just coming back from the army, just like he did. Just like his old man Junior was sent into a strange land where no one wanted him there, where you could not tell your friend from your enemy. Robert does not like to reflect too much on his boy being away and where, because it takes him back to South East Asia. So for him, it is just a relief, knowing his only son is out of that.

He will hug him and say nothing more of it, because he already knows.

Celia does not, and it is better that way, so she keeps herself occupied with preparations. She plans for his welcome home party. Invitations have been sent out to everyone on their street, even Julia, whose poor Hector did not come home. Julia has been her partner in crime the last couple of weeks and they have run out shopping and telling all the neighbors: Robert Junior is coming home.

He is coming home and she has his books bought for college for him. He is coming home and he has a room to stay in while he takes advantage of that GI Bill. He is coming home and she is ready to hear him tell her all his stories about the guys in his platoon that he shared her cookies with. He is coming home, and he is not leaving again, for a good long time.

Hours, days, and weeks of getting ready and Celia has taken care of so much before this day. She has readied herself since the day he left for boot camp. She has taken so many measures to greet her boy, and still, as the car pulls up, her heart leaps to her throat. She has done it all, and does not know what to do next.

*

For Granted

Every day she walks the neighborhood
regardless of the weather and today is no
different. Today the sky opens up and looses
endless torrents upon her and her umbrella
but still she drags the old bucket through the
streets. Everywhere she goes she stops when
she passes someone to hand her a flower
from her bucket. Some people thank her,
some people ignore her, and some look at
her like she may be dangerous. Regardless
of how they respond she smiles and tells
them she loves them.
Winston has watched her for years now
from his porch in the "nice" city
neighborhood. Observing thousands of
interactions between this young woman and
his neighbors and visiting suburbanites he
has decided she is harmless. He has received
more than his share of carnations, black-
eyed-susans, and even roses from her. She
just smiles from underneath the wide brim
of her straw hat and gives him her gifts, the
flower and the declaration, with no
expectation of reciprocity.
He would dearly love to know her story.

How she came to this place. Why she does what she does. She is intriguing and lovely and he thinks they could be friends, but something holds him back. Part of him is just like everyone else and he thinks she is probably a little crazy. Winston has had his share of crazy in his life and could do without. He feels bad knowing that he is being small-minded and a little weak. Taking some solace from the fact that she does not seem to mind he stays on his porch, sipping his iced tea. She plays no favorites, giving to rich and poor, to cops and vandals, to men and women, and old and young. He says nothing as she walks up his driveway and hands him today's offering: a daisy this time. "I love you," and she smiles and walks away.

No, he tells himself, it is better not to know her better. In a way it would be conceited. She herself is the gift to the neighborhood and to claim more than anyone else on the street would be selfish, even if they do not know what they have. He smiles content knowing that in his way he loves her back, and that will have to do.

*

Easy As Pie

There are no lines at the middle school. When he gets to the conference room it is just him and the inspectors. They patiently wait while he guides himself in with his walker and the ones that know him greet Mitch with wide smiles. He is not in a rush, not anymore. He does not have to get right back to work after casting his vote, just back to his little house where only his parakeet awaits him. Joanie has been gone for so long now. So he takes his time.

Even when he was rushed he still made the time. It was his duty, his honor, and his privilege. At least, that is how he sees it. It does not take much, just a few minutes out of his day to see what the bastards are up to, and maybe, just maybe mind you, see if there is one of them worth a damn. It is all right there for everyone to find, especially these days with the internet. Mitch dearly loves the internet. He is not a Luddite like some of the guys that visit the senior center. It seems sad to him that they do not take the time. They do not take the time to vote, or learn anything new. It is like they hate anything young, and to them any computer is young. Not Mitch though, he loves it. He loves the kids too, and not just his own. The others groan and complain but Mitch remembers that they never got out and did this one easy thing either. He watches these kids, sees how they get worked up, and he knows those two years of hell in Korea were worth it. They know what America is supposed to be about, even if he does not agree with all their ideas.

So he gets out, every first Tuesday in November, and does what he knows he is supposed to, what we all should. He does it for Jones, Boroweicz, and Smitty, the guys who only made it home in a box. He does it for these amazing kids, to lead by example. It only takes a few minutes, and it is the least he can do.

*

Calling Hours

Jane sits in the not too uncomfortable chair in the funeral home's chapel. She forces a smile through the tears for everyone who comes through the line. At eighty years and change this is harder work than she would prefer, but it is necessary. It makes the kids and grand kids feel a little more secure.

They worry so much despite the fact that she is healthier than most women twenty years younger than her.

She had Leonard to thank for that. When they were kids he insisted on hiking, biking, running, and kayaking long before those things were fashionable. "A sedentary body is a vulnerable one" he would tell her and everyone else who would listen. The irony has never been lost on her. Apparently a body in motion could be vulnerable too. At the very least the brain could be.

Bitterness works its way up her spine as his family arrives. Where were they the last fifteen years? Why did they never come around to help when this man who had helped them so much faded away? Instead she had to watch, with only their children, as her husband, who had been the terror and joy of so many of his university students forgot how to put on his socks. The man who wrote so many journal articles and whose mind was the envy of his peers slowly turned to a child in front of her and if it were not for Penelope and Ephraim, she might have gone mad.

Thinking about the twins, and how much they have had to bear, and how well they have done so, brings her out of her anger.

They have all been so strong for so long, their children as well, that this, his final passing is a sad relief. Eighty four is a long time to live, but then, Leonard did not get that. He barely had seventy years, though he lived them to the fullest.

So Jane will continue in his name, carrying his name, and see as much of the world as she can now that she can. It is how Leonard, the real Leonard, the scholar and adventurer, would want it. He would want her to experience the wonders he could not. As the last of the mourners leaves, she is already making her plans.

*

Recess And Regrets

"You don't belong here." The words echo in Ed's brain. His own voice is accusing him over and again as he walks through the old playground. So many memories and most of them had been good and that particular moment had been buried away for the better part of a decade, until last Tuesday. Last Tuesday the telephone rang, mom picked up the phone and never said a word. The phone dropped, mom hugged him, and dad walked in to tell him the news.

He was angry at himself right away, most of all for not being surprised. Nathan had always been withdrawn: a tortured, quiet boy. He never wanted to play sports or games. He never read. He never went out. He never got involved with anything at all. Nathan was not like everyone else, and the world so often let him know. It seemed like everyone told him he had no place until finally he agreed.

It has been years since that day on the play ground in the first grade. Ed was just going along with the group, making fun of the weird kid. He felt bad right way. Mom had always told him to stick up for those weaker than him and there he was being the bully. It made him sick to his stomach and he never did it again. Still, he never spoke up, at least not for Nathan.

Sullen and sometimes angry Nathan had made it so hard to do so. So while Ed never again threw fuel on that fire, he never put it out either, even though he had a reputation for getting between his fellow jocks and the "dweebs." He never included the boy. Not once had he suggested Nathan might be happy writing for the school paper, or starting a garage band. Never had one word

111

of encouragement come from him to the other, and now it never will.

The words echo in his brain and the image of the boy with the curly, black hair staring down at the ground as they were spoken is burned into his mind's eye. His head tells him that he is not to blame. His heart, however, pierces him with regret, keeping those words playing and telling him his head is wrong, and that is why Nathan is gone.

*

The Drive to Write

Jonah takes a break from driving. He has carried plenty of fares today and can take a little extra time to himself. He grabs his laptop and taps away. Jonah is going to be a writer. Every chance he gets he types and types, never stopping always pouring the ideas into his machine, when it behaves, and waiting to see what people think. He writes about anything and everything, and dreams big dreams, in the big city he calls home. Here he has a chance to make his dreams come true. He misses Nairobi sometimes, as is to be expected, but he was restless. His college education could have landed him a good job, but he was never content in any of them. When his little cousin wrote him and offered him work, he had to take the chance, so now he is here, in this city that seldom (all the press aside) sleeps. The city is like a world unto itself, like home but more so, and his job lets him explore it, gathering stories and ideas.

Some of his friends get frustrated with their fares, especially the arrogant, young, white college students. He could too, he supposes, listening to their left-handed compliments about his erudition, their woeful ignorance of his education. The assumptions that African immigrants are either poor and/or unsophisticated could make Jonah angry if he let it. The way he sees it, that is their problem.

He just gets a laugh out of it, and more stories. Fingers flying furiously over the keyboard, he spins a tale from his latest encounter, a well-meaning older woman who overtipped him so he could "send the money home." To his father the well-respected lawyer. He smiles, and writes and waves to the other drivers as they pass. They all think he is crazy and he is okay with that too, because he knows better.

He closes up his machine and turns on the

"in service light" and drives out. He drives
out to collect his fares. He drives out to
collect his stories.

*

Dodge Ball

Jesse sits in the living room trying to watch
the game. He cannot focus on it though. His
knees bounce in front of him a hundred
times a second it seems and he taps his
fingers nervously on the chair's arms. He
swallows hard and makes a deliberate effort
not to look in the direction of the stairs. He
does not want to think about what is up there
or, more importantly, what news may come
down from that bathroom.
He has too much going on now, he tells
himself. He cannot afford this. He and
Brandon just got the shop off the ground and
they are so in the red it makes him dizzy just
to think about it. It is all worth it though,
because he and his oldest friend get to
pursue their dream. Now it all promises to
come crashing down around him all because
of one night of recklessness after a wedding.
It is not that he does not love Chelsea. He
does. That is why he asked her to move in.

That is why he lets her drag him to all her friends' weddings. She is great and she never mentions at any of them that she hopes that they get their day one day soon. She encouraged him when he quit his stable, fairly high paying job when he still owed on his mortgage to open a comic book shop. She is fantastic and that is why he loves her so much, why he let himself get caught up in the passion in the fancy hotel after too much wine, even knowing the doctor told her to lay off the birth control for a month.

She walks down the stairs slowly. Jesse turns to meet her gaze and for the first time since they met he cannot read her face. Is she happy? Is she sad? What does the damn white stick she his holding say? He looks down and sees the minus sign. He tries to suppress the sigh of relief. Looking up, he knows exactly the message he sent, and how she has taken it.

*

Gut Shot

Four years of boredom. That is what high school was for Cam. Day after day of class after class, but at least he knew there was a finish line. Just four years of putting up with stupid assignments, an irritating PE teacher, and weekly visits to the guidance counselor for not living up to his potential, but it was all worth it because eventually he would be clear of it eventually he would walk that stage, receive his diploma, and be an adult. He was almost done.

Then he got the letter. His grades in economics, which he was taking for a second time, and participation in government had fallen below passing marks. He missed too much gym the last marking period, failing that as well. Three failed classes, meaning he would have to repeat his entire senior year.

All he can do know is stare at that page. His chest tightens and he feels like his entire world has come crashing down around him. He knew he was not the best student. He slacked off way too much, but still he pulled decent enough grades that he got into community college. It was not ideal, but it was a start. He knew he would do better once he was making his own schedule, once it was about learning and not jumping through state mandated hoops.

He looks at the scowl on his dad's face and the tears in his mother's eyes and he feels

like they hate him. Hell, he hates himself a
little. He hates that he did not put more into
it. He hates that he has not played their little
games for four years just so he could play
his own game later. Hindsight is twenty-
twenty though, and there is nothing for it
now. Just another year of routine, except
now he has to do it with the humiliation of
his failure.

He holds that letter tight and the room erupts
in a terrible shriek. Over and over the sound
scratches at his ears until he opens his eyes,
lying down in his bed in a cold sweat. In the
dark he looks over at the cap and gown
hanging on his door. He swallows hard, and
knows the bullet he dodged. He swallows
hard and is grateful it was just a dream.

*

His Weekly Reward

It has been a long week of sales calls,
organizing, putting out small fires, and
training people who will probably be
promoted ahead of him. Fred rubs his brow
before getting out of the car. He still has one
more day to go and the headache does not
subside. That is why he gives himself

117

Thursday nights. No nagging about deadlines at work, or leaky faucets at home. No, Thursday nights, are about what Fred needs.

He pulls his creaky body out of the ten-year old Camry and heads around the front of the building. The gaudy, pink glow relaxes Fred immediately and he hands the eight bucks to the bouncer gladly. Inside the music is louder than he likes and certainly is not his style, but then they probably are not going to play the Beach Boys here; once maybe, but not anymore. He heads straight to the bar and orders a beer, paying with a twenty and getting seventeen singles back in change. He leaves one for the bartender. He remembers when she was up on stage.

He takes his seat right in front of that stage, barely registering his image in the mirror. The girls dance for him and the other men, and the occasional woman, and slowly remove their clothes. He and the others gladly hand over their dollar bills for a closer look. What Jenny does not know will not hurt her. It is his money after all. He goes out and deals with the jerks in the office all day, not her.

After an hour he goes to the DJ and forks over two twenties for a private dance. He

has picked his favorite girl for the night.
Meeting her in the booths in back he sits in
the comfy chair as she straddles him,
writhing like a cat in heat. She treats him to
a face full of young flesh and Fred pushes
back any thoughts that this girl is his
daughter's age. It has been so long, and he
has become so adept at it, that he no longer
needs to actively rationalize that Taylor
would never end up like these girls.
No, this is just his little treat. His well-
earned reward, and it is nobody else's
damned business. He gives himself this, and
will keep on doing so, and he will not feel
guilty, even a little.

*

The Long Way Around

Snow whips into his face, driven by the
harsh, lake winds, but Pete just buries his
head deeper into his hood. He walks along
the boardwalk, cautious with every step,
because falling into the ice-cold river is
definitely not on his list of things to do
today. Then again, leaving his nice warm, or
at least not freezing, house to go out and get
momma's cancer sticks was also not on is to

do list. Still, that is what he finds himself doing, so he just keeps on keeping on, gloveless hands buried deep in his pockets. He takes this way because he knows no one else will be down here, not this time of year. Pete's a quiet boy. He always keeps his head down, he always keeps out of trouble. No mean feat in this all to mean neighborhood. People on this side of town have been forgotten. The only time anyone notices is when a corpse shows up in public, and even then, so long as they belonged there, well, only so much attention is paid.

When you feel forgotten you feel worthless, so you no longer care about what happens to you. You sell rocks on street corners, or yourself. You pick up bad habits and maybe hurt others to pay for them. Mostly you just hurt yourself, because why not? At least that is something you can control. Sure the "right" people will tell you to put down that forty, or go wait in line at the jobs office. They say that because they don't know any better.

Pete knows better, even if he chooses to stay clear of trouble. He doesn't judge anyone. Gram let him and momma move in with her when momma got sick, so they live here, with the forgotten people. They live here and are ignored until it is too late. They live here with people who Pete would rather walk an extra mile to avoid in the bitter, lakeside cold than to risk an encounter gone wrong.

There's no fixing it, so why worry? He just does his best not to get caught up. Some day momma will be so sick they'll have to move her into a home. When that happens, he can move on. Until then, he takes the long way around, his hands in his pockets, and head buried in his hood.

*

Neuro-Chemical Confluence

A mile a minute the ideas fly at her. She can do it all she is certain of it. She just needs to keep the ball rolling, keep her head of steam, keep up, keep going, keep pushing through, and keep bouncing around. Her hand grips the pen as she scribbles on her journal haphazardly and she barely notices the mess of bowls, pans, whisks and other implements of creation around her. It does not matter. All that matters is that she keep her momentum.

Stephanie is convinced she has solved it.

She knows what to do now. All she needs to do is, well, do. Do anything to maintain an active mind. Give in to this endless creative impulse, this sleepless urge to move without any clear direction. Direction does not matter. Direction is the enemy. If she sets a direction, she will get into a groove. If she gets into a groove, it will wear her down, and she cannot let herself get down again. No, this is how she is going to beat it this time.

The doctors were wrong. She does not need meds. She especially does not need Lithium. All they do is leave her in a fog. They make her worse, not better. Stephanie wants to be better. She knows her "sickness" can make her better. Manic-depressive, bi-polar, or whatever it is they want to call it this year; it is a gift, not a curse. That is what she has convinced herself of. This time it will work for her not against her. This time she will not sink into that pit of tar that drags her down at the end of an "up cycle" because she will stay up by keeping the ideas going. That is the plan, but then she has been so creative in the past. It is only a matter of time until the cookies are burnt, until the rhyme is broken, until one thing leads to another and she is so angry at it all and she

just cannot make it work. It is only a matter
of time before she can only see the failure.
When that happens her anger at her failure
consumes her, and she can see only one way
to correct it. There is only one way she is
guaranteed to never fail.

*

After The Fire

Dishes remain piled in the sink, bottles
tipped over on the counter, and two chairs
stay on their backs in the dining room.
Ashley has only had the wherewithal to put
the Thanksgiving left overs in the fridge and
has been staring at a now warm glass of beer
for three hours. The perfect holiday get
together ruined because her little sister
cannot get her act together.
Why Shawna thought she would just keep
her mouth shut is a mystery to her. Ashley
has always been the one to tell anyone, no
matter how much she loves them, exactly
what is on her mind. It is tough love and if
you cannot handle it, tough luck. The truth
hurts sometime, but it will also set you free.
So when Shawna said she was quitting her
steady gig in market research to go back to

school and get her masters in nutritional anthropology, whatever the hell that is, she had to say something.

She could not just let her sister, the one she has been taking care of since they were put in foster care together, throw away another promising career. Shawna has always done this. She has always been impulsive and irresponsible, never just settling down and settling in the way Ashley has. It was for her own good, but the poor kid, if you can call a thirty-three year old woman a kid, just cannot see it that way.

So she exploded, right there at the dinner table in front of everyone. She did not swear, and Ashley is grateful for that. Shawna is a bad enough example without doing that in front of the kids. She did, however, scream, and slam the table and said many cruel things about Ashley. She insinuated that her older sister lived a shallow and meaningless life, and Ashley returned fire with more observations about her kid sister's choices. No one else said a word. They were all too afraid, and once Shawna was out the door, Craig sat their, jaw dropped, while Ashley cleared the table. None of them get her, or the sacrifices she makes to keep them happy,

but she will keep on doing it, and keep on
speaking her mind, consequences be damned.

*

The New Christmas

Christmas is weird this year. At least, that is
what George thinks. He sits next to his dad
in the car, even though he isn't big enough to
sit in the front seat yet, as they head to
Grandma Miller's party. He looks over at
him and can see he is just pretending to be
happy. Everyone is pretending to be happy,
like nothing is different, and little, nine-year
old George Miller does not know what to
think about it.

At Nana Frey's party they thought he did not
hear them. The kids were sent to open their
presents and play with them and the grown
ups sat around the dining room table talking
away. They talked about football, and the
President, and something called the
economy. They talked about Mama and
Uncle Jimmy too.

They tutted and wondered how he could do
that to his own little sister. George doesn't
know what "that" is, but he figures it has
something to do with why Mama and Uncle

Jimmy are in jail. They visit Mama a lot, but no one visits Jimmy. That makes George sad because he is his favorite uncle. He always bought the coolest toys and played video games with him and took him to ball games. He had the coolest car, not a beat up piece of junk like Dad's.

So this Christmas they have to do without Mama, and Uncle Jimmy. This year they don't have as many decorations because he and Dad had to move into a new, smaller, apartment. This Christmas he has to stay at Nana Frey's because Dad has to work. Dad has to work whenever he can because he had to quit his old job so he could be home when George got out of school.

This Christmas is not as fun as the old Christmases. He thinks about this as they pull up to Grandma Miller's house, the back seat full of presents they bought at the thrift shop because they could not go to the mall this year. He does not like this new Christmas at all, and cannot wait for Mama and Uncle Jimmy to get out of jail so it can go back to the way it was.

*

Praying At the Overhead

Jason strides into the Large Group
Instruction room, a box full of syllabi under
his left arm while he carries his laptop case
in his right hand. His brown hair is thinning
and turning white in places and the forty-
five minutes he spends at the campus gym
before lunch is not quite enough to fight off
the paunch on his mid section.

Still there is a spring in his step as his new
students sluggishly slip into their seats in the
amphitheater like room. Each year, since the
first year he was ABD he has told himself
that he will not make any judgments about
his students, but it is hard to not recognize
certain types after twenty-four years
teaching Political Science.

Right off he notices the students in the front
row: the dozen above average students
trying to make an impression and the two or
three truly exceptional ones that want to be
in the thick of it. Two rows back are the
good students with little to no self-esteem.
He will have to work hard to pull them out
of their shells. After that are the "just get me
through the semester" students, followed by
the "mom and dad want me here"s. He notes
them, but does not judge. After four years it

will be entirely likely that one or two from the front and back rows will trade places. This class is an easy one: American Political System. They all likely have opinions already tucked neatly into their minds and will defend them rigorously. He spots a freshman girl, not too shy, not too open in the second row and recruits her to pass out the syllabi. Quietly she does so as he hooks his computer up to the overhead projector, ready to show them what is ahead.

He lives for this, even after two decades. Some of his peers think he is too enthusiastic, too romantic, but he sees this as important work. He hesitates to use the word "sacred" but it is the closest that comes to his love of teaching. He shapes young minds, and therefore the future. Even if he is wrong, for him there is no greater thrill than watching a "Eureka!" moment in a student's eyes. He turns on the projector, displaying an image of the Declaration of Independence (give them an easy first day he tells himself) and putting on his bifocals asks "who can tell me what this is?"

*

After The Flood

The rain patters softly on the sidewalk as
Hunter crosses the park on her way home.
She likes walking in the rain, it cleans the
world, and she has always enjoyed the smell
of wet grass. There is something comforting
about it. Not that Hunter needs comfort right
now; at least, she does not think so. If she
thinks about it for a moment, she realizes
she does not know exactly what she thinks.
Jake said he loved her, and she has no
reason not to believe him. He is a sweet boy.
He's always so polite, to her and her mom.
He helps them with keeping up the house
while Hunter's dad is in Afghanistan. He
listens for hours when she tells him how
much she misses her daddy. He is perfectly
happy, most of the time, to just cuddle. This
afternoon was different though. This
afternoon they did "it."
She is not that kind of girl, whatever kind of
girl that is. Jake is the only boy she has ever
kissed, and only the second one she ever
held hands with. Somehow, Hunter has
convinced herself that makes it different,
better somehow. Others may think
differently, but this is how she feels, she
thinks. It is just that Jake seemed in such a

hurry for her to leave when they were done. He said he forgot about his social studies project and needed time alone to concentrate on it. He would not lie to her. Somehow, for some reason, Hunter is not sure it matters one way or the other. She is unsure whether to be happy, sad, scared, or even indifferent. She feels guilty that she liked it, even though she and her mother have always been open about that kind of thing. A smart girl, Hunter wonders how these doubts have crept into her head.

The rain eases, leaving her with the soothing scent of the grass. Hunter sees her house in the distance, her mom waiting on the porch. In the next few minutes she will decide whether or not to tell her mom. For better or worse she has passed a marker in the road of her life, and though she still does not know how to feel, she does know she cannot go back.

*

Planting the Seed

Michael refuses to cry. He will not give them the satisfaction. He sits in the cruiser with the handcuffs pulling his shoulders back uncomfortably and the knots form in his back screaming at him to cry, but he will not do it. He does that, and they win, all of them: the shop owner that called him in for loitering even though he was just waiting for his friends. The cops win. The lily-white brats from the high-priced housing tracts at the top of the hill win.

No one says anything about the cans of spray paint in their hands. No one will ask if they were the ones who drew the giant dick on the back wall overlooking the trailer park. They only care about the red-brown paint on his skin. Michael always knew it would be like this. His dad said it is not like that anymore but grand dad, Uncle Jamie, everyone else knows. Everyone in the trailer park knows better. Poor is worse than rich, and brown is worse than poor.

It builds up in the Arizona heat, the hate, anger, fear and frustration. It pushes up through his lungs, through his neck and tries to force its way out his eyes but he will not let it. It is his rage, and he refuses to give it away. He refuses to give in. He will not end up like Cousin Jamie Junior in maximum security because he kicked back, because his rage ruled him.

He pushes it down and locks it down. In his

head it is something physical and real and he lets it grow in his soul as the cops and shop owner point and laugh. They take their sweet time and it just gets stronger. This cold thing taking root in Michael (not Miguel, because his dad is a self loathing tool) coils around his heart and he grips it tight. He will bide his time. He will be stronger than this.

Then and there, feeling a chill despite the triple digit heat, Michael makes a decision. He will beat them, beat them all. He will not let them transform him into a stereotype. He will not just be a demographic, forgotten on some PO's desk. He will be remembered, and they all better pray, when he is done, when his metamorphosis is complete, he is more merciful than them.

*

A Different Kind of Coming Out Story

"That's nice." That is all mom said. Lenora chews on that, just a little. She wonders how to interpret it. Months of anxiety, days of worrying leading up to today, and hours, right through dinner, wondering how she and dad would react and all that is said is "that's nice." Part of her wants to be angry. She wants to believe they are being dismissive, or smug. She remembers how she could be so, in high school, with her "believer" class mates, and after a while, she just thought that all her fellow atheists just "got it."

Then she met Jeremy. He turned all her misconceptions about Christians on their heads. His acceptance of her lack of belief, and of others' beliefs left her without the armor she covered herself in for so long. Days turned to weeks, turned to months and before long she began seeing the world through the same lens he did. She opened her heart and felt the divine love. It did not matter if others felt it. It did not matter how others lived their life. All that mattered was being open to it. Jeremy did not use his faith as a crutch. He never judged, and in fact, was open to all sorts of interpretations of the Bible. To him his faith, all faith, was a deeply personal thing, and while he withheld judgement, as he thought everyone ought to, he was saddened by those who presumed to know the mind and heart of God without opening their minds and hearts.

So she did just that, and felt it. She felt it despite being raised by two atheist parents:

her mom the physician, and her dad the philosophy professor. She expected some kind of fight, but instead got "that's nice." That, and a discussion, over doing the dishes with dad that everyone has to walk the path that is best for them, so long as they do not hurt anyone else. He said he did not get it, but he did not have to. It was not, he told her, his place to get it. All any of them had to understand is their love for each other. He winked as he demanded to "meet this boy who converted my little girl" before hugging her. Her family loves her no matter what, and Lenora knows that is very nice indeed.

*

A Storm Subsides

The rain tapers off, with the lighting fading on the horizon. The thunder is now just a whisper in the distance. It is drowned out now by the sound of windshield wipers. Calvin focuses on these things. He thinks about the road, the storm washed fields, the smell of the cigarette he just finished, and anything else that keeps his mind of why he is driving to his friend's house this time of the day on a Sunday.

He had told Carolyn to get someone else to
be their couple's therapist. He was to close
to it all, but he knew she was right. Lance
would not go to anyone else. So Calvin was
stuck with it. He tried, he really tried. For
six months he has been listening to them,
putting all his training to work,
remembering not to take sides, remembering
not to over-correct in Carolyn's "favor."
He could see it though. He could see Lance
sliding into old, bad habits. He
recommended he see a psychiatrist, and that
was when they guy who used to defend him
from the bullies in high school started
pushing them both away. He closed off in
session. Lance had become more and more
distant, and this evening Calvin got the call.
Now his friend is locked in his bathroom,
his wife unable to draw him out. They both
fear the worst. He has shown the signs for
weeks, months even. It was one of her
complaints when their sessions started, that
Lance would not get the help he needed.
When it became obvious that it was true,
Calvin asked him in private, and made
things worse.
He pulls up the long driveway to their farm,
his heart in his throat. He wonders if she
should have called the cops, he wonders if

they are too late. Calvin begs a god he has claimed to doubt that his friend is OK. "Please" he pleads, "give us all a chance to make it right." As he approaches the house his relaxes a little as he sees Lance and Carolyn, an overnight bag at his side. He steps forward as Calvin steps out of his car. "I'm ready to go now." Lance forces a smile, and Calvin checks directions to the nearest psych ED on his phone.

*

Controlled Crash

Everyone is gone now. The party is over and DJ is all alone in his hotel room. They came together for the conference ostensibly to network, but they all knew each other anyway. That is all these things are to them: a chance to blow off steam after a hard quarter of working. They spend their days, their nights, their weekends and holidays building their companies all for a shot at the prize at the end of the never-ending race. They have no illusions, especially DJ, they are just cogs in the wheel of industry. He knows his place.

So he makes the most of it. He has a nice

condo back east and a sweet, if not too flashy ride. Best of all he has a reputation of being the life of the party. He is the hook up at all these get-togethers. DJ knows all the right people, or if he does not, his "friends" back home do. He always knows how to score, no matter where the conference is. That is why the party is always in his room. They come for the wild ride, and he is in the driver's seat. It does not matter that he cannot just hit the sack when he wants to. He has to keep up his rep. So he bumps more lines, pops more pills, and downs more shots than anyone else. It is no big deal. They all need it. They all earn it. That is true for DJ most of all.

He has it all under control. He has to tell himself that as he straightens up a bit. It gets intense sometimes. It got intense this time. No denying it as he uses a hotel towel to clean sick and blood off the toilet seat. Some people can't handle it, but DJ won't blame them for that. Not everyone has his level of cool. It isn't easy.

It is worth it though. He is convinced of it. He is convinced as he watches the sun rise over the plaza and realizes he won't be getting any sleep after all. It is all good though, he has a cure for that, and he grabs the bottle of little white pills. He pays no mind to the bags under his eyes as he looks into the mirror before stepping into the shower.

*

Bliss on the Mirrored Stage

Kate rubs the liniment into her knees before putting on her jeans. All around her younger women are either getting dressed after work, or undressed for work. Some of them love her, some of them hate her, and some of them think nothing at all of her. Most think she is jealous of them, which is silly, since she was young once too. She may not have the perfectly smooth skin of these youngsters, but she still has her moves, and her banter.

She is not deluded. She knows many of these girls, the ones who can actually dance, and who have not been harassed by gravity just yet, make better tips than she does now. Still she's not in it for the money, not really. She has her own business, and a successful one at that, but the conversation with the customers at her counter is not as fun as the conversation here. Kate loves that she can still get the boys to part with their bills, even though she is well over forty. She will never say how well though, and teasing about that makes her a little more.

No more nose candy or even booze for her. She does not begrudge anyone, but that just is not her scene anymore. Sometimes a girl will ask advice about that sort of thing and she just tells her "sweetie, ya gotta figure that out for yourself." It was fun, for a while, but it gets in the way, at least for her. If it works for you, Kate has no problem with that.

Occasionally she will let herself feel protective of these girls, especially the ones who feel like they have no other choice. "Dance because you love it" she tells them, "otherwise you won't make dick, and you'll hate yourself." Some even listen. Everyone has their reasons though, and again, she won't judge.

As she leaves they all wave goodbye like they were best friends forever, even the ones who hate her. She will see most of them next week: the down and out, the up and coming, the high school drop-outs, and the PhD candidates. They all dance for the boys, and some girls, and make their money, or have

their fun, and Kate knows it doesn't matter
why.

*

Building Calluses

It gets easier. It has to get easier. Everyone
else tells her it does. It has only been two
months, she has to remember that, but
Stephanie cannot see any improvement.
Maybe she is being impatient. Maybe she
should be, when their idea of improvement
is not caring so much anymore. At least,
that's the way she sees it.
She is young, she knows, but not naive.
When she took the job as nurse in an inner
city school in an undeveloped country, she
knew she would see things that would upset
her. She sees the malnutrition, the abuse,
bruises from angry parents, and split lips
inflicted on each other. The addiction
though, that she was not ready for. Nor was
she ready to see STD's in 12-year-old girls;
so very many children scarred so early.
Every night she goes to bed crying. She
feels like she has made a terrible mistake but
cannot go back. At least once a day she
wants to yell at the teachers and other aids

for being so calloused. They go through the motions, doing what they can. It is clear they care, they are so gentle and kind to these kids, but their lack of outrage outrages her. How can it possibly get easier? How can anyone get used to this?

Every day is a tour through some new hell. Each child is a reminder that the world is a cruel place. Stephanie came here because of her faith, and each night, she puts out the lights feeling like she has lost a little more of it. She has no way of knowing how to make any sense of it: what has happened here, what their efforts gain.

Little by little her French improves, and she gets to know these kids better. At first this makes it harder. She falls in love with them, but Stephanie knows she cannot rescue them all, if she can rescue any of them. Then she meets the parents, and grandparents, those who know what real horror looks like, those that remember the bombs and the guns. She sees that they have walked a harder road than she could ever imagine.

Maybe they cannot make a difference. Stephanie does is still not certain. She does not know if she can develop those calluses, but slowly realizes, they are worth it.

*

First Taste

Her heart races. Hands full of fliers,
surrounded by strangers, television cameras
off to the side and Simone just wants to see
him. He is the reason she came here. He is
the reason she made that phone call asking
how she could help out with more than just a
few bucks. She watched him on the internet.
Listening to his speech she knew that he
could make a difference, and through him,
she could too.
It is so strange the difference a year makes.
In high school things that matter did not
matter to her. She wanted her license, her
friends, her boyfriend, good grades to get
into a good school so she could get a good
job; whatever that means. Politics was other.
It was a strange world filled with people she
was told not to trust. Like her parents, her
siblings, cousins, aunts, uncles and friends,
all she saw was the stage, and like too many,
did not care one way or the other.
Then she went to school, in more ways than
one. Classes taught her but conversations
with her friends educated her. There was a
world beyond her immediate needs and it

was not what it could be. Sometimes it seemed like it would never be. That was until she heard him.

So she wanted to help, any way she could. She knocked on doors, held signs at rallies and shouted along with the rest. Letters to the editor poured out of her mind through her fingertips and on to emails. Arguments with her dad got heated, but Simone knew he would understand. This man had waked a sleeping giant inside her, and before long she realized she was not alone.

At the cluttered, cramped campaign headquarters she met so many people. Some just wanted a pay check, some truly believed, and some needed him in office, to fight for them. Regardless of why, they all fought for their man, and it felt good. They were part of something important and Simone was proud, of herself and her new companions. Some of the people she hands fliers to toss them to the ground. It does not bother her. She was like them once too. A shrug of the shoulders and it is time to move to the next person on the street. They will win, she can feel it, and then, on to the next fight.

*

Real, and Ugly, and Oh So Hilarious

Steppan laughs. He tries to hide it, or at least
make the reason for his laughter less
obvious, but he laughs all the same. He
laughs as he guides the witless Americans
through his beautiful St. Petersburg. His
English is very good, having spent a summer
with his uncle in London. He hears all their
little conceits. He knows what they think of
Russia, and how much they think they know
about his Motherland. He is not particularly
patriotic, but something about them brings
that out in him.

It is good money, showing them around, and
he does not even charge them too much
extra to show them the "real" parts of the
city like they ask. They are silly children so
eager to experience the world. So ready to
see parts of another country that they would
stay away from in their own. They do not
want to look like tourists, which is why
Steppan laughs. He laughs and tells his
friends at the bar.

"Yes, of course the working man drinks
here." He tells them, and laughs that they
seem not to realize that the Socialist

Republic ended twenty years ago.

They want to get their hands dirty, or at least pretend like they know what it means to do so. If they really wanted to do that they could have done it home. They could have helped the poor back in America, it is funny how they all seem to think the rest of the world does not know what happens in their country. No, they do not really want to see the ugly side of things; they just want to feel like they have.

So he just takes them to any regular bar. He makes sure they never really see the ugly. God knows Steppan has avoided those places. He knows what happens, here, in Moscow, in Warsaw, Paris, London, and New York. There is ugly everywhere and anyone with any sense avoids it. These Americans have no sense though.

That is why he takes their money. He takes it and keeps them safe despite themselves. He takes it and shows them the "real" St. Petersburg. He takes their money, and he laughs.

*

The Last Mile is the Hardest

Gwen looks at the ground as she walks from
the bus stop. She does not want anyone to
notice her. She certainly does not want to be
recognized. She is dressed nice, if plainly. A
simple, light-pink tee-shirt and blue jeans
bought at a thrift shop. Her hair is pulled
back in a pony-tail, a style she almost never
wore in the past. Ambling down the street
she realizes it is doubtful anyone knows who
she is. They will though, when she walks up
to the house.

It has been months since she walked up to
that house. The last time she walked up that
side-walk was months ago. That is not
entirely true. It has been longer. The last
time she was here she crawled and stumbled
up the sidewalk, taking a detour to the
willow in the front yard to vomit up half of
what she drank that night. Her father rushed
out to help her inside while her mother
shook her head. He begged her not to go out
the next night, but she did anyway.

Her friend had been even more intoxicated
than Gwen, so half in the bag; she took the
other woman's keys and started the car.
They did not even get out of the municipal
parking lot. Fortunately she was not going

fast enough to hurt anyone when she drove the big Buick into the rear corner of the bank, but the cops were right there.

Now it has been six months of jail time and rehab. Six months of reflecting on how she lived her life. Mostly six months at least, as Gwen realizes she spent the first week or two in angry denial. That was before hearing everyone else's stories. Friends crippled, families left in economic ruin and one woman who has to live with the knowledge that she killed a little boy. Gwen knows how lucky she is.

She knows and is ashamed. She lifts her head to see that walkway and those steps and is afraid. They will never trust her, she believes, and they are right to feel that way. It is the only place she has to go, however, so she puts her head down, and puts one foot in front of the other.

*

Front and Center

It must be some kind of mistake. That is what Lawrence keeps telling himself. He was not supposed to be here. It was someone else's time, someone else's place, and he is absolutely convinced that they would not have felt what he is feeling now. He knows their stomach would not be twisted in a millions ways. They would stand up, stand proud and be confident that their bladder was not about to give out on them.

Someone had to do it though. The lead had to go and get drunk at the cast party and punch his understudy in the face. Everyone joked with the director that it was what you get when you put cousins in the same cast. Said director shot back that in twenty plus years of Community Theater he had never seen that happen, and everyone agreed that the two were out. That meant, of course that they had to cancel the show.

No one liked the idea though. Everyone volunteered to take their place, but there was only a week to learn the part. They went around for three hours when Grace mentioned that both of them had been rehearsing with Lawrence. She made sure to take a picture of the look on his face with her phone when it sank in what she was getting at. It was a great idea, Lawrence had to admit it. He knew the part. He loved the show. There was just the tiny problem of his never having been in any named part before. Lawrence had always been happy in the chorus, part of the show but never noticed. He did not like being the center of attention, and now he was about to be thrust into the limelight. His knees are week as he walks out to center stage and delivers his monologue. He hits his mark, remembers every line, and his timing his impeccable. When it is done his heart is racing. It was not as awful as he thought it would be. Just three more performances and he can be done. He will be safe in the background again, loving the theater without being noticed. Enjoying things on his terms, the way he likes. For now though he will not disappoint anyone, no matter how uncomfortable it makes him.

*

In One Breath

Chastity panics. Her legs will not move as she looks out the garage window hoping and dreading mom or dad finding her and Billy. He is lying on the ground and she is sure he is turning blue. His eyes are wide and tears are rolling down his temples as he grabs his throat. It was not supposed to be like this. She was bored. No one was paying attention

to her. No one wanted to play with her even
though it was her eleventh birthday party too.
No, they all wanted to play with her perfect
twin sister, Vicky. They wanted to spend the
day with the girl with the perfect hair,
perfect eyes, perfect smile and perfect skin.
Vicky was not covered in pimples like
Chastity. They weren't even real twins.
"Fraternal" is the word Vicky would use.
Chastity didn't even get to be the smart one.
So when Billy said he had something to
show her she went along with him to the
garage. At first she thought he wanted to
play "doctor." She had done that with their
cousin Kevin once. It was icky and weird.
Instead he grabbed an empty can of whipped
cream, stuck it in his mouth and pushed the
tab.
"Try it," he grinned, "it's fun."
So she did. He was right. It was fun. It made
her head go light and she felt like she was on
a roller coaster without being on one. She
giggled as her eyes rolled back in her head.
This was way better than watching everyone
make a big deal about her perfect sister.
Billy did it again, only this time he did not
hand her back the can. Instead he acted like
he was choking. His face turned colors and
he thrashed around a bit before falling to the

cement floor. Chastity went to her knees and begged him to tell her what to do, but all he did was stare at her.

Now she was frightened half to death. She was sure he was going to die. She should get an adult, she knew, but then everyone would know what she did. Frantically her head turned back and forth, looking for someone, all while her legs betrayed her. She wanted someone to find them, and she was scared to death they would.

*

Stolen Time

Leonard waits as the guard processes his paper work. That is how life is behind bars, always waiting for your betters to tell you when you can move, even as they are sending you on your way. Three years, six months, and four days. That is how long he has been here. That is how much time they have taken away from him for something he never did. He could have been almost done with college by now, but some scared white lady fingered him in a line up, and that was all it took. He had no good alibi, other than "I was at home eating pizza." All they had

151

was her, but that is all it took.

Three years, six months, and four days. That is how long it took them to find her watch and her purse. That is how long it took to track it to the man who sold it from his pawn shop to the man who actually took it. Not that they ever convicted him. Not that they ever gave him that speedy trial he was promised in his American History class. No, they sat on her ID and his lack of alibi and had sweet eff ay to hang on him, but it was enough to keep him in jail, not having the money to even get a bond. It all went into paying for his first semester.

They stole that from him. They stole three years of his life, just like that dumb punk stole her purse. She got her purse back, and her money, and her watch. What does Leonard get back? Does he get those three years, six months and four days? The community activists say he can get big money, and maybe he can, but he cannot get that time. They tell him he can get angry, like he needs their permission.

He is angry, and nothing is going to fix that. All he can do is try to pick up where he left off. Maybe the money will help, if he even gets it. He is not sure he wants it. What he wants, what he really wants, more than

anything is to look her in the eye and ask
"why?"

*

If Not Now

Salt and copper fills his mouth as the
stinging pain burns James' lips. He smells
metal and his eyes begin to sting. His knees
are week and his arms are heavy but he
refuses to go down. He has walked away too
often and he refuses to now. Everyone
knows James is the one who puts his head
down and takes it. It started in kindergarten
and has continued up until now, in the
seventh grade.
To be honest, he did need to stand up.
Something just snapped. Nathan slapped
him in the back of head so James turned
around and shoved him. Nathan's friends
formed a circle, James' slinked away. He
does not care though. He does not care as
fists crash into his ribs and mouth. He does
not care as Nathan pummels his stomach.
His vision blurs and his head swims and still
he stays on his feet.
Swinging wild and fast, only one in ten of
James' blows land. Nathan's friends laugh at

153

the awkward boy. None of them sees the rage in their friend's eyes. He was challenged by this scrawny loser, and none of them knows how angry he is; no one in the yard to, except for James. James feels it with every jab and swing. He tastes it in the blood running from his nose. James is angry too, almost as angry as he is happy.

He should not be proud. He knows that. Mom taught him to turn the other cheek, but that cheek had been slapped too many times. So he his proud. He may hate it later. As Nathan's blows slow down James has no idea what will happen next, but he is certain the worst of it is behind him. More people gather around as the bigger boy's arm wraps around his head. James cannot hear what he is shouting and does not care. He only knows he is still on his feet and the crowd around them is getting bigger.

His friends have returned, along with half the class. Other students are chanting Nathan's name, and James' own pals are silent, but they all know now. He has nothing to be afraid of anymore. His ears burn as flannel rubs against them and all he can see is the ground. Neither of them sees the principal, and neither cares.

*

Cost-Benefit Analysis

A sunny Saturday morning beckons through the window of Clarence's home office but he is busy finishing his end of quarter reports. The work needs doing. The work keeps him and his family, a wonderful wife and three amazing kids, in their comfy suburban home in a good school district. The work lets him save for their college education. The work lets them afford for everything they could want or need. The work is a small price to pay to know they are cared for.

He does not give it much thought, his earlier exchange with his youngest, the bright-eyed child smiling up at him with the football in his hands and then frowning as he explained to the boy that he is busy. One day he will understand, and he even does a little now. A shrug and an exaggerated, resigned nod, the kind only a five-year old can pull off, and the boy is outside with his elder siblings, running around. The work is a small price to pay to know that they can do that.

It was only supposed to consume a couple of hours, but two turned to three, turned to four. Summer fun called to too many of his subordinates and their work was passable, but shoddy. Not worth an immediate lecture, but they will remember come time for their reviews. The work is a small price to pay for the luxury they enjoy.

The reports are bleeding into a fifth hour now, and Clarence knows there is work left to do. He has chores afterward, the sort of tasks his wife does not have the time, or raw muscle for during the week. She does so much day in and day out to keep the family healthy, physically, mentally, and emotionally that mowing the lawn is the least he can do. The work is a small price to pay to keep it all going.

Then he sees her across the street. Janice Mayweather, attorney, head of the PTA, chair of the community theater, and all around power mom. She is playing hide and go seek with her kids. Clarence looks out the side window to his children, puts the computer in sleep mode, and remembers what the work is paying for.